OKLAHOMA STARSHINE
THE MCINTYRE MEN
BOOK THREE

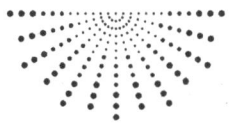

MAGGIE SHAYNE

All rights reserved.

No part of this publication may be sold, copied, distributed, reproduced or transmitted in any form or by any means, mechanical or digital, including photocopying and recording or by any information storage and retrieval system without the prior written permission of both the publisher, Oliver Heber Books and the author, Maggie Shayne, except in the case of brief quotations embodied in critical articles and reviews.

PUBLISHER'S NOTE: This is a work of fiction. Names, characters, places, and incidents either are the product of the author's imagination or are used fictitiously. Any resemblance to actual persons, living or dead, business establishments, events, or locales is entirely coincidental.

Copyright 2015 by Margaret S. Lewis

Edited by Jena O'Connor, Practical Proofing

Published by Oliver-Heber Books

0 9 8 7 6 5 4 3 2 1

❦ Created with Vellum

CHAPTER ONE

You wouldn't have known it to look at him, with three soused cowgirls hanging from his arms, but Joey McIntyre was bored. And charming these ladies into letting him drive them home was nothing more than his duty as part owner of the Long Branch, Big Falls Oklahoma's most popular claim to fame, after the falls themselves. This year, though, the nearby Holiday Ranch was rapidly becoming another.

The player piano was tinkling an 1890s version of "Joy to the World," and hidden projectors beamed tiny illuminated images on every wall; Christmas trees, Santas and stars.

A soft-handed sweetie stroked his face, or tried to, and managed to poke him in the eye. "You're a real hero, giving us a ride home, Joey. You gonna come in for a nightcap?" Her knees bent and she sank floorward. Joe tightened his arm around her waist to hold her upright, and she beamed up at him, wafting beer breath that would've scared the jingle bells off a reindeer at twenty paces.

"Yeah, Joe, you have to come in," said the one on the other

side. She was trying to make herself tall enough to nuzzle his neck, but kept tipping off her stilettos.

The girls' night out had taken a turn for the rowdy by the fifth or so round, and when one of the girls reached for her keys, Joey knew it was time to step in. It was times like these he wished Darryl Champlain hadn't quit his job as their bouncer-slash-head of security to go back to full-time songwriting.

The third hayseed honey shuffled along behind him, her hands on his shoulders, head kind of bouncing along against his back because she could hardly hold it upright. She mumbled something but he wasn't sure what.

They all wore skin-tight jeans so low slung they gave even scrawny girls a muffin top, and blouses that showed varying amounts of cleavage.

"I should've cut them off," the new waitress said. "I should've cut them off at four rounds." Her name was Heidi, and it fit. Blond hair and blue eyes so round she always looked either scared or surprised.

"I think they had a head start before they got here," Joey said. He didn't want her to think she was in trouble. "It's a bar. People are gonna drink. Will you check to see if we got all their crap from the table?"

Nodding and gnawing her lip, Heidi hurried away. One of the girls listed left, taking him and the other two with her, but he managed to keep from hitting the floor, then got them all upright and back on track for the garland-draped batwing doors again.

He looked back at the bar, not wanting to leave the place unattended, but as usual, his brother Jason was nowhere to be found. He was spending all his time at his fixer-upper outside of town or over at Sunny's Bakery these days. Not much help running the saloon anymore. But he did spot Rob, taking a shift behind the bar while his country-fresh Kiley sat on a saddle shaped barstool, making doe eyes at him.

He caught Rob's eye, inclined his head, and his brother hopped over the bar and jogged up to him. "You uh, sure do have your hands full there, little brother."

"Yeah. Can you hold down the fort while I get them home?"

"I can." He assisted by taking Joey's keys from his belt loop, and putting them into one of his hands, which he couldn't move because it was holding up a drunk girl. A drunk girl who was smiling sloppily up at him and trying to bat her lashes. Looked more like she had something in her eyes. "You gonna be okay with all this?" Rob asked.

"Lucy's place is the closest. I'll drop 'em off there, make sure they get inside."

"And not go inside with them. Cause they're drunk."

Joey sent him a look. "You think I'm immoral or just stupid?"

Rob shrugged. "Hey, you're the billionaire bachelor of Big Falls, pal. I'm just looking out for you." He eyed the women, each of whom was pawing Joey in her own way. Suzy Jennings, Betty Lou's niece, was petting his back like he was a cat. Geri Starbuck (no relation) was trying to lick his neck, but couldn't reach.

"Just help me get 'em in the truck, huh, Rob?"

Nodding, Rob turned toward the exit, just as a redhead came through the batwing doors, stopped about three feet in front of Joey and looked him right in the eyes.

He was so surprised to see her that he let go of the girls on either side of him, and took a step toward her. All three cowgirls landed ass first on the hardwood floor.

"You dropped something," she said with a sarcastic lift of one brow.

"Emily?"

"Hello Joe. Haven't changed much, I see."

"I don't know what you...oh, this? No, this isn't what you... Shoot, how the hell are you? It's been what, four years?"

"Something like that."

Rob cleared his throat and Joey remembered his brother's presence, looked his way, saw him nod at the three on the floor as if to remind him of his unfinished business. But Rob's new bride stepped in. "Rob and I will get these three home so you can catch up with your...friend." Then she extended her hand. "Kiley McIntyre. Welcome to Big Falls."

Emily smiled, her face softening. She was still beautiful. More elegant than he remembered. Her cheekbones seemed more pronounced, her eyes, more deeply set than before. Then again, she'd only been twenty last time he'd seen her....

Outside his father's Texas mansion, in the grotto behind the waterfall, among the ferns and honeysuckle, beneath a midsummer moon.

"Emily Hawkins," she said. "Good to meet you, Kiley." Then she added, "Hello Rob."

"Good to see you again, Em. How are you?"

"Great. Wonderful." Joey thought her eyes didn't match her words, and while her lips tried to turn themselves upward, it wasn't a smile. It was some kind of hidden pain, trying to impersonate one.

Kiley helped the girls to their feet, one at a time. "You're gonna ride in the back of the pickup. You're gonna sit still and shut up and hold your vomit until we get you home. Understood?"

They nodded at her, and no wonder. She was sweet and young and freckled, but she sounded more like Vidalia just then.

"You puke in the truck, you're cleaning it with your toothbrushes. So just don't." She took a girl's arm in each hand and marched them out the door. The third was clawing at Joey's jeans, trying to pull herself to her feet.

Rob grabbed her under her arms and hauled her upright, then steered her toward the door. "Come on, let's go." He sent Emily a nod, glanced at Joe and said, "I'll be back to help you close up."

He nodded, but wasn't really paying attention. They all got out into the parking lot, and the place went quieter. Patrons stopped muttering about the spectacle and went back to their own drinks and conversations.

For a minute he and Emily just stood there, staring at each other, and he felt the years fall away. He felt like they were kids again, all wrapped up in each other, hearts pounding with the all-consuming power of young love.

She blushed, then she seemed to tear her eyes off him, taking a slow look around the saloon. "So you're a bar owner now."

"Part owner, with Jason, Rob and Dad. Lately, though, it's mostly just me."

"Whole family's in town, then?"

"Mom's still in Texas. She got the place in the divorce. Remarried. She's pretty happy."

"Who wouldn't be?"

Was her tone sharper just then? "Come on in, I'll show you around." He put a hand on her arm, and she shied away from it, but walked further inside.

"You serve food, too?" she asked.

He nodded and walked her between the pulled-back, red velvet curtains that marked out the border between barroom and dining room. An evergreen tree took up about four tables worth of space near the front windows, but it was worth it. It bore only twinkling multi-colored lights, at the moment, and filled the whole place with that pine-scented holiday feeling. The ornaments would come later.

"We've got a chef that'll make you weep," he said, walking her slowly around the dining room. The chairs were already up on top of the tables. "It's really a touristy kind of place. We have dinner theater, bad guys and saloon girls, fake shoot-outs and poker games gone bad." He nodded toward the source of the happy holiday music. "That's an original player piano. Dad had it restored."

"Cute," she said, but the tone didn't match the word.

He looked at her face to see her expression and got stuck on her eyes. Emily's eyes had always been impenetrable, as dark green and shiny as wet lily pads. And they still were. "So the tourists don't mind the alcoholic cowgirl hookers?"

He frowned at her and wondered if life had turned her mean. "They're not so bad, Em. Just some local girls, best friends their whole lives. Lucy's getting married next weekend. I think tonight was a pre-bachelorette party bachelorette party." He looked toward the big front windows, the parts not blocked by evergreen boughs, and said, "Tell you the truth, I think it was good for her to let off some steam. Wedding planning is stressful."

"I wouldn't know," she said, which made him dart a quick look at her ring finger, left hand. Bare as ever. Why did that send a surge of knee-weakening relief through him?

"I would." He said it just to see her reaction, which was to look down real fast, and catch her bottom lip between her teeth. "Robby just married Kiley in September. I thought the Brand gals would kill each other before—"

"Brand gals?"

He pulled a couple of chairs off a table, set them upright. "Dad married Vidalia Brand, mother of five remarkable females. Turns out Vidalia was his first love, and one of Vidalia's daughters is his."

"You have a sister?" she asked, sitting down and widening her eyes at the same time. Why did the question seem disproportionately important?

"That I do. Her name's Selene." He hadn't sat down yet. "You want a drink, or something to eat? Ned's gone home, but there are always snacks around."

She crossed one leg over the other. Her jeans hugged her calves, then vanished into the tops of fake fur boots, all the rage with the local girls. "How's your coffee?"

"Best in town." He shrugged. "Well, next to Sunny's." He went to the curtain, leaned into the barroom and caught Heidi's eye. "Bring us a pot of coffee?"

"Sure, boss."

"You okay out here for a few minutes?" he went on, giving the barroom a quick scan. Only about a dozen folks remained, half of them playing cards, the others looking pretty docile and content.

"If I can't, I'll holler," she said.

He nodded and took his seat at the little round table for two. He could barely believe Emily was actually here. "I looked for you at your dad's funeral," he said. "We all did. Henry was…well he was like family to us. We loved him, you know."

"I saw you there," she said. Then she shrugged. "I just couldn't handle…people, you know? So I stayed out of sight until everyone else left. Said my goodbyes in private."

"It was a little more than that, though," he said slowly. "You didn't even call. Some stranger came by to tell us what happened. I rushed over to check on you, and you were just gone. I called and called–"

"I know."

"I was worried about you. Which, given the self-centered jerk I used to be, is saying something."

"Used to be?" she muttered, half under her breath. She wasn't looking him in the eye.

"Sorry, that's not the answer we were looking for. The correct response was, 'Aw, you weren't all that bad.'" He was joking.

But Em didn't so much as crack a smile. There was something in her eyes, something big, and dark and inexpressibly sad. He reached across the table, laid his hand on top of hers. She jerked a little, like she wanted to pull it away, but then stilled again and just let her hand rest there, all stiff and twitchy and cold.

"What brings you to Big Falls, Emily?"

"What brought *you* here?" It was delivered as quick as an Ali counterpunch.

Just then, Heidi came in with a tray and unloaded it onto the table between them. Then she poured from the big brown earthenware coffeepot, filling two man-sized mugs with longhorn skull logos.

"Thanks, Heidi."

"No problem." She set the coffeepot on the table, between the matching cream and sugar holders. Then she took a lighter from her apron pocket and lit the candle inside its cactus-shaped globe made of green tinted glass. When she left, she freed the red velvet curtains from their tie backs. They fell together, silent as snow, muting the sounds from the barroom and leaving them in complete privacy.

"Where were we?" he asked.

"You were telling me why you moved here."

"Right. Well, long story short, Dad got sick. We thought we were gonna lose him. He came here to see the love of his life one last time and to build the Long Branch. I think it was supposed to be a legacy for Jason, Rob and me."

"He's okay, though?" she asked.

Joe nodded. "Wound up finding a daughter he never knew he had and a cure he never even expected." He gazed past her briefly. "It was kind of miraculous the way it all went down. Christmastime and all."

Emily stopped with her coffee mug halfway to her lips, blinked three times, rapidly, then seemed to steady herself and took a sip. "That *is* good coffee," she said. "So you came for your dad and just never left?"

"There's something about this town," Joey said, gazing again toward the windows. "You'll feel it, too, if you stay around here long enough. How long did you say you're here for?"

"I didn't," she said.

He frowned at her, wondered why she was being so secretive. "Did you ever become a vet, like you always planned?"

"You remember that."

"I remember everything." Especially the night he'd caught her and her girlfriends using his father's pool. They'd climbed the fence and sneaked in. He'd heard the splashing, gone out to investigate, and there she'd been. Emily, in a bikini, looking like a young man's dream come true. He remembered the way the water was all beaded on her smooth skin, and the way the pool lights lit up her dark green eyes, and how he forgot his aquaphobia for a few seconds while he was staring at her.

He was staring again. She was staring back, but she seemed to realize it and tugged her eyes away. "I did, actually," she said, and her words jarred him out of the memory.

It took him a minute to remember his question. Oh, the vet thing. And then her answer lit up in his brain and he said, "You did? That's great, Em! So do you work for a clinic or—?"

"I have my own practice," she said.

He sat back in his seat, blinking at her, impressed to his core. "Hell, I don't know why I'm surprised. Everyone always knew you'd do amazing things with your life. Graduated high school early and already had an associate's degree."

"All those college classes they offer in high school these days. It's not that hard."

"You had your BA at eighteen. That's hard. You must've sped through vet school at the speed of light, too."

She shrugged, lowered her eyes a little.

"So where is it? Your practice?" He would love to see where she worked, he thought. To see what she'd built, what she'd done since with her life he'd seen her.

But more than that, he wanted to know why she'd left him.

"Anywhere I want." She leaned back in her seat, and for the first time, seemed to relax a little bit. Sipping her coffee, clearly enjoying it, she went on. "It's a mobile practice. I have this tricked-out van with everything I need inside. I call it the VetMobile."

The way she said it, it rhymed with Batmobile, and he got it immediately, and grinned. "Do your patients shine a spotlight into the night sky when they need you?"

"Yeah, with a vet-shaped silhouette in it."

"Va-va-voom, woman. If it's shaped like *this* vet, it's gonna be a very confusing signal." She rolled her eyes at his flattery, but he went right on. "Men will flock to the light, only to find..." He left it unfinished, to let her fill in the blanks.

She shrugged. "Anything from a mare about to foal to a constipated guinea pig."

"That's not a real case," he said.

She lifted her brows and nodded, and he slapped his thigh and laughed. "That's great, Emily. That's really amazing. You did your father proud."

Her smile died. "I like to think so."

"So where's your territory? Where is home for you these days?"

"I've been in New Mexico for a while. I like it there."

He nodded. "I've been there. Beautiful country."

"It is. But it's never felt like home to me." She sat up a little straighter again. "This saloon ownership agrees with you, doesn't it Joey?"

He looked around the place, realized he was proud of it. "It does. Jason and Rob are both pulling out, bit by bit. They've got their own irons in the fire, and this isn't their passion. Rob married Kiley, and they bought a ranch together. He raises Thoroughbreds and she caters to the local kids with special events for every holiday. Dad wants to retire, show his feisty bride the world. So I'm taking on more and more around here."

"And you resent it," she guessed.

He flinched when she said that, but had to admit, that was the guy he used to be. "I expected to resent it, when I first realized what was happening, but I don't. I really don't. I kind of like it, as a matter of fact. Lately, I keep getting ideas to expand the place, make it better." He shrugged. "Who'd have thought?"

"Yeah, who'd have thought." She looked at him a little oddly for a long moment, and then quickly glanced at her phone. "God, we've been talking for an hour. I've gotta go." She rose, slugged the rest of her coffee back and put the cup down.

He got up, too. "Coffee's on the house," he said.

"I pay my own way, Joey." She fished a couple of singles out of her jeans and put them on the table. "It was…it was good to see you again."

"It was fantastic to see you," he said, feeling almost desperate. She couldn't just leave. "Are you um…do you have a room somewhere? I've got the whole second floor, if you need—"

"No, I'm good." She looked up at him, paused, nodded as if she'd made a decision. "I'm staying at the B and B."

"B and B?"

"Yeah, um, Peabody's? Out on Church Road?"

"Oh, the boarding house. Ida Mae's place." His spine sort of dissolved in relief. She wasn't leaving…yet. "Okay, good. I'm glad you're…sticking around for a while."

She nodded. "So…yeah. I'll probably, you know, see you."

"Yeah, you will," he said.

He was holding open the curtain by then, and she turned and walked across the bar, through the batwing doors and then right out the bigger doors to the outside.

Joey resisted the urge to jump up and click his heels. Hot damn, Emily Hawkins, right here in Big Falls.

All of the sudden, Joey McIntyre was the furthest thing from bored.

∼

Joey McIntyre hadn't changed a bit.

That was what she'd thought when she'd walked into the tacky cowboy saloon. Hot hometown honeys dripping from him like a rich widow's jewelry. He'd always been a player. She oughtta know, he'd played her like a fiddle.

A willing, stupid, naive, starry-eyed fiddle. Yeah, that. Until he drove the bow right through her heart.

"Doesn't matter." She walked up to her van and unlocked it with the key fob. As always, before she got in, she took a second to love the thing. It was glossy black with dark burgundy swooshes. And there was a very Bat-signal-like logo on it, unless you looked close enough to notice it was a winged-V in a white oval. White lettering followed the curve, proclaiming it The VetMobile. She opened the door and got in, running a hand over the two-tone "pleather" seats that matched the paint job. Even the car seat in the back matched. You know, underneath its layer of crust, composed of Goldfish crumbs and apple juice.

There was no reason, she told herself, to believe was anything but what he'd always been—a spoiled, rich, self-centered playboy who didn't have a care in the world for anybody but himself. Worse yet, he liked it that way.

She imagined his face when he'd first looked at her. God, he was still just as beautiful to her as he'd always been. The tall lanky frame, those long arms that used to wrap all the way around her and then some. And his sweet face, and chocolate brown eyes and little boy lashes. God she loved looking at that face of his. Always had.

That face could charm the moon out of the sky.

She started the van, flipped on the headlights, and then the heater. It was chilly tonight. And then she backed carefully out of the gaudy saloon's parking lot and headed back onto the winding, narrow road. It turned into Main Street once it hit the village. She didn't have to go that far, though, hanging a right onto Church Street, and then past the church little white church with the big red doors, and on up to the B and B—make that boarding house—where she was staying.

It was a pretty Victorian in a violet shade so subtle it seemed white at nighttime, and its elaborate trim work was decked out in pine green, minty pink, and baby blue. The sign that swung from a wrought iron holder had matching wood-trimmed edges, all scrolled like the trim on the house, and read Peabody's Boarding House. Ida Mae Peabody's holiday decorations were far more understated than most of the others in Big Falls. She had a single white electric candle in each window and a giant wreath on the front door. Period.

Emily shut off the van and hopped out. The front door swung open before she even reached it, and Ida Mae herself stood there, holding a cherub with burnt gold curls on her hip. But the angel quickly wriggled free and ran toward the porch steps. Emily reached them first, and scooped her up before she could fall.

Matilda didn't even notice her brush with disaster.

"You're supposed to be asleep, young lady!" Emily said, closing her eyes and just inhaling the smell of Tilda's hair. The greatest smell in the known universe.

"I waked up!" Matilda said.

"I'm sorry I wasn't there. I had to see someone."

"Was it Santa?"

"No, honey. It wasn't Santa."

Matilda pouted. "But we have to find him and tell him so he'll be able to find me!"

"And we will. I promise."

"Tomorrow?" Tilda asked.

"Yes," she promised. "Tomorrow."

Tilda hugged Emily's neck a little tighter. "I love you, Mommy."

"I love you, too, baby."

CHAPTER TWO

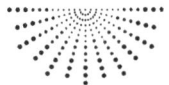

For the first night in two weeks, Emily's dreams didn't take her back to the pediatrician's office the day everything changed.

Tonight, lying in a strange bed in a strange town, with her little girl sound asleep beside her, Emily's dreams took her back a lot farther, to that big, fancy pool with the water that was always just the right temperature. It always had its chemicals perfectly balanced. The water was always the perfect azure blue, and algae wouldn't dare try to invade. She knew all that because her father was the guy who kept it that way.

Emily's father had been groundskeeper to billionaire JRJ McIntyre since Emily could remember.

Taking midnight swims in the pool had been her own little bit of rebellion, she supposed.

She was floating there again, in her dream. Lying on her back while the cool water kissed her cheeks, staring up at the starry Texas sky and refusing to think about school or goals or anything at all.

And then his head blocked her view, leaning over and staring down at her.

She was so startled she went under, and came up sputtering, only to see Joey McIntyre with a look of terror in his eyes. "You okay?" he asked.

She pushed her hair and the water out of her face. "Fine. Were you about to jump in after me?"

"Only if I absolutely had to."

Then she looked around. "Sorry about invading your pool without permission. I figured no one would mind, it being the middle of the night."

"I don't mind," he said. "It's not like I use it."

She swam over to the marble steps to get out. He met her at the top holding out a towel, and she wrapped up in it. "It's warm!"

"I turned on the heater. Sat over there and watched you for a few minutes while it baked."

She frowned at him. "That's kind of creepy, Joey."

He shrugged. "I've been watching you every night. You and your friends. I think you guys get more use out of our pool than my whole family does."

Her eyes widened. "Why didn't you say something, then?"

He shrugged. "I don't know. You were having fun. I didn't want to scare you away." He nodded toward a little table, tucked in behind some rose bushes near the waterfall. "I have some wine coolers."

"Congratulations."

He smirked at her. "Come on, I thought it would be nice. We used to be friends. Gosh, we were like *best* friends from like, seven or so to fourteen. I don't even know what happened after that. Why did we stop hanging out?"

She shrugged. "You hit high school and realized you could have any girl you wanted because your last name is McIntyre and you're passably good looking."

"Passably?" He held a hand to his chest. Then he shook his head. "I think what happened was that you hit high school and realized you had the biggest brain in the building and could take every course in the place and still graduate early," he said. "And you're wrong about me. I couldn't have *any* girl I wanted."

He looked at her when he said that, and her cheeks got hot. She reached for the wine coolers. They were in an ice chest on the flagstone patio, and she pulled out two, handed him one, and twisted off her cap.

"You had your private school friends. They didn't fit in with my crowd."

"You didn't have a crowd, unless you mean your books." He shrugged. "How's college going? You a Ph.D. yet?"

"Not yet."

"You ever take a break from all that learning, Emily?"

She held his eyes. They were the most beautiful eyes she'd ever seen on a man, rich lustrous brown with thick, dark lashes. "That's kind of what I'm doing out here. Taking a break. Floating and looking at the stars."

"And drinking wine coolers with an old friend," he said. He extended his arm, tapped the rim of his bottle against the rim of hers.

"How about you?" she asked. "What are you doing with your time?"

"Enjoying it, mostly," he said. "Studying business so I can step into my father's corporate universe and earn my inheritance."

"Is that what *you* want to do, though? Or what your father wants you to do?"

He frowned at her like she was losing it. "It's what he wants, and I'm more than happy to go along with it. I mean, look at the way we live." He waved a hand at the opulence that surrounded them.

She nodded, took another long pull from the bottle.

"What about you, Em? Are you doing what you want or trying to live up to *your* dad's expectations?"

She sighed heavily. "Sometimes I'm not so sure. I mean, I want to be a vet. I know that. But all this accelerated program, genius IQ stuff is...it's starting to feel a little heavy to carry."

"I get that. You're the golden child. He talks about you like you're gonna be president of the world in a year or two."

"Yeah, that. It's a lot to live up to." She emptied her bottle, and without thinking, reached for another. "He doesn't have much, though. I mean he's a groundskeeper."

"He's *our* groundskeeper. That's gotta be like the best job in the groundskeeping universe."

"Arrogant much?"

"No, I didn't mean...okay, I did. Dad loves him, you know that, right? And your dad, he's an artist, too. I mean, look at this place."

"Yeah. Thanks." She started to get up.

He held up a hand. "Don't, don't go. I miss you, Emily. Life is...it's getting all complicated. You're right, my father is pushing me to do what he wants. I don't fight him on it because I don't have any better ideas. I don't know what I want out of life." He heaved a big sigh. "Mom and Dad are splitting up."

She sat back down, stunned. "I'm sorry, Joey. That has to be hard on you."

He nodded. "I just wish we could go back, you know, to when things were simple. Remember trying to catch the frogs down by the koi pond?"

"I remember you almost drowning in the koi pond, is what I remember," she said.

He got all tense and looked away.

"You haven't gone swimming since, have you Joey?"

He shook his head. "Water makes me feel...panicky." Then he reached for his second wine cooler. "This stuff, on the other hand, seems to be taking the edge off my evening."

"Mine too," she said.

So they stayed up, and they drank the wine coolers, and

they got stupid drunk, and they made out. And after that, they were together, every day and every night of that hot Texas summer.

~

Joey woke before the alarm went off and bounced out of bed, feeling eager for the day to come. He headed straight into the bathroom with a happy spring in his step, looked into the mirrored medicine cabinet door. The guy looking back at him wore a mile-wide grin. And when he tried to straighten his lips, they kept pulling right back up again.

Okay, no point fighting it. Emily was back, and he was ridiculously happy about it. Even though she'd been less than friendly last night, there was only one reason he could think of for her to be in town. Him.

And he was happy about that.

He probably oughtta be pissed. She'd disappeared without a word, after the most passionate ten-week romance that had ever existed in the known universe. But her father had died, right out of the blue. And everything had changed.

Henry Hawkins had worked for the McIntyres since Joey was just a little boy. Losing him was like losing a member of the family. And Emily, she didn't even tell them herself. Just up and vanished, moved out of the cottage on his family's estate, and took off without so much as a goodbye.

He'd damn near gone out of his mind worrying about her, especially when she wasn't at the funeral.

Now he knew she had been. She could've at least talked to him. Something. Anything.

He'd got a postcard in the mail a week later. She'd gone back to New Mexico early, she wrote. Their summer fling had been fun. But he shouldn't make anything out of it.

She's broken his damn heart. Shattered it.

To be honest, he'd never really recovered. Maybe first loves were like that.

But she was back. Hot damn, she was back! And as much as he told himself he should be good and pissed at her with for walking away like she had, or at least cautious about setting himself up for another fall, he couldn't feel anything but overjoyed. Maybe he was about to get a second chance with her.

He showered, and he shaved, and dressed in jeans and a western-style button down denim shirt. It was December, and even in Oklahoma, it could get downright chilly. Even snowed every now and then. He put on his best boots and headed down the stairs.

When he got to the bottom, he was greeted by heavenly scents of fresh-brewed coffee and Jason's french toast. He hurried to the bottom and saw that his brothers were at the table closest to the giant Christmas tree, with heaping platters of deliciousness in between them. There was a third place set for him.

Jason looked his way with a grin. "Well now, little brother, you sure do look spit-shined this morning."

"You shaved," Rob noted.

Joey rubbed his baby-smooth chin and said, "It was starting to get itchy." Something was up, no question about it, but the french toast was too much to resist, so he walked into the bear den, sat down and started filling his plate. The butter was already melting into each slice of toast. He stabbed four pieces and dropped them onto his plate, then thrust his fork into the sword fight going on over the sausage and emerged victorious with two patties as his prize.

"Rob tells me Emily Hawkins is in town," Jason said.

"Yep." Joey dumped real maple syrup over everything on his plate.

"How are you, uh...feeling about that?"

He had a mouthful of food, so he didn't have to answer. Instead he gave a careless shrug and filled his coffee mug.

"Did you know she was coming?" Rob asked.

"Unh-uh," he managed, and shook his head in case it was too french-toast muffled. Then he swallowed and followed up with a big gulp of hot coffee.

"You okay, Joe?" Jason asked. "Cause that girl did a number on you back then, the way I recall."

Rob was nodding. "Our happy-go-lucky kid brother turned into a morose, short-tempered brooder for a while there."

"A year," Jason said. "Mom wanted to take you to a shrink."

Joey rolled his eyes and stabbed another oversized bite. But when he brought his fork toward his face, Jason put a hand on his wrist to stop him.

"You can talk to us, Joe. We know how it was. She was your first serious crush."

"She wasn't a *crush*." Damn, he'd blurted that too fast. He set his fork down, leaned back in his chair, and gave each of his brothers a searching look. They watched intently, apparently expecting him to pour his heart out while sobbing into his breakfast at any second.

"You two are turning into a pair of snooping, meddling females. I think you've been spending too much with our recently-acquired sisters. I'm completely over that. It was more than four years ago."

They sighed, sent each other knowing looks, but shrugged and surrendered.

His sense of relief was so immense, Joey thought he could've floated off the chair. So he ate some more, and they stopped asking questions. They talked about easy stuff, like Rob's Holiday Ranch and his horses, three of which were carrying foals, and Kiley's Christmas hayrides with free hot cocoa. She was selling blown-glass ornaments, holiday recipe books, and solar powered Christmas lights in the smaller barn, among other holiday items. She'd bought them in bulk, wholesale, for a song. He didn't even want to know how she'd managed it. Turned out former con artists made great entrepreneurs.

When he'd tucked away all the food he could hold, Joey wiped his face with a napkin and said, "I'm glad you boys are here. You haven't been doing a hell of a lot around this place, and I—"

"Yeah, I know," Rob said. "I'm sorry."

Jason nodded. "Me too, Joe. You're taking on way more than your fair share, and we—"

"No, it's fine. Fact is, I like running the place. I think it might be...I think it might be my thing. You know?"

His brothers sent surprised looks at each other.

"I want to buy you both out." He pushed back his chair and got up. "But I haven't yet, so I need you to step up until I do. Run the place for me so I can take tonight off?"

"What's going on tonight, Joe?" Jason sounded like he was afraid of the answer.

Joe smiled. "I plan to be busy." He dropped the napkin on the table. "Clean up your mess, boys, and lock up when you leave." He sauntered, all the way to the front door, pulling his jacket on as he went, and humming.

~

"Cakes need frosting. That's why we have syrup." Three-and-a-half-year-old Matilda Louise was about to pour said syrup over the two remaining bites of already-soaked pancake on her plate.

Emily managed to grab the pretty glass decanter in the nick of time, and said, "Baby, you've got plenty of syrup. Look, it's formed a little pond in the middle of your plate."

Frowning deeply, Matilda Louise crossed her arms over her chest and huffed. "I want more syrup and I wanna do it myself!"

If she'd had a camera on her, Emily would've snapped a

photo just then. Her little girl was cute when she was mad, and too smart for her own good. Her gold and honey curls framed her face and decorated her forehead, and her round baby cheeks were as pink and plump as apples. A plastic tiara with pink "jewels" sat crookedly on her head.

Not for the first time, a wave of remorse washed over Emily for never telling Joey he had a little girl. Sure he hadn't wanted her. But if he'd ever seen her... Who could look at Matilda and not love her?

"Honey, look how the syrup on your plate made a little puddle there? It's almost like a swimming pool for your pancakes."

Tilda looked. Her brows rose, and then a slow smile spread across her face. She stabbed an inch-sized square of pancake, lifted it way up over her head, and said, "Go swimmin', pants-cake!" Then she smashed it down into the syrup puddle, and sticky droplets exploded in a dozen directions.

"Oh, Matilda...."

"Don't you worry about that one little bit," said Ida Mae, coming through the gorgeous hardwood double doors. She'd served them breakfast in a glass enclosed sunroom, all soft yellow paint and bright white trim, and those antique doors with the oval glass insets. After serving them, Ida Mae had left them to enjoy their incredible breakfast in private. She reappeared with a silver coffee pot, held it up with a question in her eyes, behind a pair of Mrs. Clause specs. "Refill?"

"Yes, please. And you have to let me help you clean up."

"Nonsense." She filled Emily's cup. "You did a very good job on your breakfast, Miss Matilda," she said. "And so..." She opened her palm to reveal a tiny red and white striped candy cane.

Matilda's eyes widened. Then she shot a quick, worried look at her mom. "Can I?"

"Sure you can."

She snatched the candy from Ida Mae's soft palm so fast she knocked the syrup decanter over, but Emily caught it in time, met Ida Mae's eyes, and they shared a smile. Then she turned back to her baby girl. "What do you say?"

"Thank you very much," she said, pronouncing every syllable with exquisite care. "And for the breakfast, too. It was delicious."

"Well, I'm glad you enjoyed it. It's been a long time since I've had a little girl to cook for."

"Don't worry. It will be lunchtime before you know it."

Ida Mae laughed out loud, then turned as the doorbell chimed. "I'll go get that." She hurried away, leaving the coffee pot on the table.

"I'll go get that, too!" Matilda scooted off her chair and went running behind Ida Mae.

"Tilda, baby, it's not your house." Emily chased her toddler, catching up just as Ida Mae opened the front door to reveal tall, lean, handsome Joey McIntyre standing on the other side. And she froze, because the moment she'd been dreading and trying unsuccessfully to prepare for, had arrived. She wasn't ready. She hadn't decided how to tell him, what to say, how to explain…

But she didn't have a choice. She met his eyes, and he met hers, and then he looked lower and saw Matilda Louise standing in front of Emily, gazing up at him with her big brown eyes, and Em realized all at once that they were his big brown eyes, too.

~

Joey almost fell over when he saw the miniature version of Emily standing four feet inside Ida Mae's front door, with Emily behind her, hands on her tiny shoulders. There was no question the little girl was hers. She had Emily's copper and honey curls, and her elfin nose. What a stunner she was, tiara and all.

He managed to regain his powers of speech, and said, "Good

morning, Miss Ida Mae. I didn't know you had a real live princess staying here." Then he sketched a formal bow. "Good morning, your highness."

The little girl giggled. "I'm not a *real* princess," she said.

"You sure do look like one."

Tilda smiled, and turned to hug her mom's denim clad leg.

Emily stroked her curls. "Hi, Joey. This is my daughter, Matilda Louise. Tilda this is Joey. He's an old friend of Mommy's."

The little girl released her mom's leg, gripped both sides of her own flouncy skirt, and bent her knees in what he thought was supposed to be a curtsy. Joey's heart melted. He had a thing for kids, and this one was a something special. "Nice to meet you."

"Very nice to meet you, too."

"Come on in, Joey," Ida Mae said. "Why don't you all visit in the sun room? I'll bring a fresh coffee cup."

"It's this way," Matilda said, and she grabbed Joey's hand and took off. He didn't have much choice but to follow. As they jogged past Em he sent her an apologetic smile.

He thought he heard her mutter something but couldn't make it out, and then he was being pulled into the sunny former back porch of Ida Mae's grand old house. The porch had been converted into the prettiest, sunniest little room ever, long and narrow, with a wall of window panes facing her back yard.

Ida Mae intercepted them before they could sit down at what had clearly been their breakfast table. "Over here, by the windows," she said. "Nice and clean. I'll clear that mess up and get right out your hair."

She put the big silver coffee pot on the clean new table, added fresh cups, and a glass of juice for Tilda. Then she made quick work of clearing the other table.

Joey said, "That's a nice swing set you've got out back, Ida Mae. Is that new?"

"New in June," she said. "My boy Travis built it when he came to visit."

"That's amazing," he said, admiring the wooden set and nodding.

"It has a climbing wall," Matilda told him. "I climbed almost all the way up it already."

"That's probably higher than I could get," he replied. "Ida Mae, remind me to get Travis's number from you before I leave."

"You want a swing set built?" she asked, amused.

"Among other things. There's nothing for kids at the Long Branch, and there's plenty of room. I was thinking a miniature golf course, a big swing set, maybe a go-cart track. And definitely a paintball target range."

"My goodness, those are some big plans. I'll jot down Trav's number for you, hon. I'd love it if he had an excuse to spend some more time in town." She nodded at Emily. "Just let me know if you need anything." Then she headed out, carrying all the dishes and things from the breakfast table away with her.

Joey smiled and looked back at Emily. Then he frowned. She looked as tense and tight as he'd ever seen her, lips pressed into a small, straight line, eyes worried, and maybe damp.

He frowned at her, then looked at the little girl again. "Do you want to show me how you can climb the rock wall?"

"Yeah! Can I, can I?" she asked her mom. She was already on her feet and looking eagerly toward the back door.

Emily nodded. "If you'll wear a jacket."

"Why! It's not cold. I'm hot already." She stomped a foot, crossed her arms, and Joey had to bite his lip to keep from laughing out loud.

Em told him with her eyes not to dare laugh at her daughter's defiance. He got the message. "I'm wearing *my* jacket," he said. "It looks nice out, but there's a bite in the air."

"A bite?" Tilda widened her eyes.

"That just means the air is cold, honey," Emily said. She was already taking a jacket off the back of a nearby chair.

"Oh, is that your jacket?" Joey asked. "I love Dora, too. So does my little niece Dahlia. She's five. How old are you, Tilda?"

"I'm almost four."

"You're three-and-a-half."

"That's almost four."

"I'll tell you what, my niece Dahlia, she would be jealous of that jacket."

Smiling, Tilda took the jacket from her mother's outstretched hands, ducked away when Em tried to help her put it on, and wrestled herself into it. It took about four times as long as it would have taken Emily to put it on her, but Joey knew the deal. She was at the I-can-do-it-myself age.

She got the jacket on, then opened the glass-paned back door and hurried across the deck, down the steps and over to the swing set to begin climbing.

Joey held the door for Emily, who had filled both their cups and was carrying them outside. They sat on the steps and watched Matilda climb. Every few seconds, Tilda checked to make sure their attention was still on her.

"You didn't tell me you had a little girl," he said. "She's beautiful, Em."

"Thanks. I um...I was planning to introduce you to her. I just wasn't quite ready yet."

He frowned. That was an odd thing to say. And she seemed so tense and...wait a minute. The little girl had said she was almost four, and he started doing math in his head. "How close did you say she is to turning four?"

He watched her face. She closed her eyes.

"April," she said. "She was born April thirtieth."

"April." He counted backwards from April, nine months, and the bottom fell out of his stomach. "Then she was conceived in July. That same July we..."

"Hey! You stopped watchin'!" Matilda called.

He stared at the little girl, then at her mother again. "Emily?"

Emily opened her eyes and met his. "Yes, she's yours."

He felt like a spiderwebbing fracture spread over his entire world in that moment. He had a little girl. He, Joe McIntyre, was a father.

And Emily had kept her from him for three years and seven months. He stared from the child to her mother and back again.

"Why in the name of God didn't you tell me?" And then he frowned, and his anger heated up to a low simmer in his gut. "Where the hell do you get off, not telling me I have a little girl?"

"You don't have a little girl. I do. And I'm telling you about her now."

He got up to his feet, glaring down at her.

She got to hers as well. "You're furious. I didn't expect that."

"What *did* you expect?"

"I expected you wouldn't care any more now than you did then. I expected you'd assume this was some kind of a shakedown and demand a DNA test. Actually I still expect it, once the shock wears off."

He just gaped at her. "What...what...what kind of a man do you think I am?"

"Same kind you always were. Selfish, spoiled, and aspiring to be the world's richest playboy."

"For love of God, Emily."

"Mommy?"

"In a second, Tilda." She looked at the little girl, then at him again. "You should go. Cool down, digest this. We'll talk again."

"You're damn straight we'll talk again."

With that, he strode across the back lawn to the little girl, crushing his anger down inside him with every bit of will he owned. He looked at her, there on the fake rock-climbing wall with the sunshine making her hair look like spun gold. Reaching out, he touched a soft curl, and his throat closed up.

"You're about the prettiest little girl in the whole state of Oklahoma, you know that?"

Her smile lit her whole face.

"I have to go right now, but I want you to know, I'll be back. And if you need help with anything, anything at all, ever, I'm your guy. Okay?"

She nodded, frowning, maybe sensing his overwhelming emotions. Emily was coming right up behind him, all nervous and jerky, like she thought he might snatch her or something.

"I do got one problem," she said softly, and very seriously.

His heart melted. "What is it?"

"I'm afraid Santa won't be able to find me on Christmas Eve."

He wanted to pull her off the rock wall, hug her to him, and never let go. But he didn't want to scare her. To her, he was just a stranger. Because of Emily, she didn't even know she had a daddy.

"Well, you're in luck, little lady. Santa's a personal friend of mine." He glanced back at Emily to be sure she would hear every word. "I'm taking my niece and two nephews to see him this afternoon, as a matter of fact. I'll take you too, if you want."

"Joey, I don't think that's—"

"Please, Mommy? Pleeeaase, can I go see Santa?"

He turned to Emily. "He's in the park in town. You can be there too, if you want. It's not a big deal."

She looked at him as if his words confused her. But finally, she nodded. "Okay. All right, we'll come."

He nodded. "I'll meet you at the diner by the park at four." Then he leaned in closer, almost to her ear, and whispered, "You'd better be there, Emily. You try to take off with my child, and I'll follow and I'll find you. And you know I have the resources to do it."

CHAPTER THREE

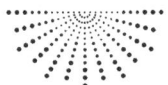

*A*fter Joey stormed around the boarding house to the front and took off, his oversized truck roaring like an agitated bull, Emily stood there, trembling from her head to her toes and seething.

How dare he? How dare he call Tilda *his* child and how dare he use his filthy money to threaten to take her?

If he thought he could push her around like that, he'd better think again, because—

"Mommy, I don't feel very good."

She spun to face her little girl, realizing she'd taken her eyes off her for at least thirty seconds. Disaster could have rained down. But the only disaster was that Matilda was leaning on the rock wall with her hands on her tummy. "I think I had too many pants-cakes."

Em's own stomach tied itself into a knot and she hurried to Tilda, feeling her forehead, looking into her eyes. *It's just the pancakes. She ate four of them and a cup of syrup. That's all it is.*

Please God, let that be all it is.

Scooping her little girl up, she carried her inside, holding her close. "I'm gonna find us a doctor, baby, and make sure you're okay."

"But I still get to see Santa with the nice cowboy, right?"

Emily nodded. "Right." She needed to make nice with Joey McIntyre and his family, regardless of their treacherous, heartless, money-grubbing ways. She needed them.

Matilda needed them.

Ida Mae saw her as she moved through the house toward the stairs, and came hurrying behind them. "Is everything all right? Did she fall?"

"Belly ache," Emily said.

"Too many pants-cakes," Matilda moaned with an extra helping of drama.

"I'm sure she's fine, but um…is there a local doctor or clinic? You know, just in case."

"Sure is, hon. I could throw a stone and hit it. You want me to give Doc Sophie a call?"

"If you could just get me the number…"

"Of course. Take her on upstairs, honey, I'll jot it down and bring it along."

Emily carried her girl up the stairs, into their beautiful two room suite, and set her down on the claw footed sofa. Its fabric was red, swirled with pink roses and vivid green vines. A flat screen TV was hidden behind the beautifully tooled wooden doors of an armoire, so as not to clash with the Victorian theme of the place. She opened those doors and worked the remote to find a cartoon. By the time she had a pillow tucked behind Matilda, a blanket over her, and a digital thermometer in her mouth, Ida Mae was tapping on the door.

"Come in," Em called.

Ida Mae did, just as Emily pulled the thermometer out of Tilda's mouth and took a look. "Ninety-eight point four," she said aloud.

"You know, she looks perfectly fine to me," Ida Mae said.

"Better than you do at the moment." She leaned in and handed her a three-by-five index card with a phone number written on it.

Emily took it, nodded. "I'm sure she's fine. Thank you, Ida Mae."

"Are you fine, though?" Ida Mae was looking from Matilda to Emily over and over, her eyes wise and curious. "You have reason to react this strongly to a tummy ache, Emily?"

Em looked up from the phone number card, caught the woman's probing eyes and said, "I'd better make this call. Thanks, Ida Mae."

Taking the hint, Ida Mae nodded and said, "I'll leave you to it, then. You just call me if you need anything, though. Anything at all."

"I will. Thanks again."

Nodding, she left.

Emily looked her baby over, running her palm over her little forehead repeatedly, pushing her curls back. "Does it still hurt, honey?"

"Yes. Awful." She thrust out her lower lip to emphasize how bad she felt.

Em got out her cell phone and tapped in the number. The phone rang. A cheerful female voice answered. "Dr. McIntyre's office. How can I help you?"

"M-McIntyre?" She blurted stupidly.

Matilda sat up on the sofa, her eyes going wide. "I gotta go potty! I gotta go!"

"I-I'll call you back," Emily said. She ended the call, tossed the phone, grabbed her little girl and ran for the bathroom. She set her on the toilet, and Matilda Louise scrunched up her entire face, bared her teeth, and passed a loud, long fart.

Then she giggled and giggled and giggled. "That was nasty!" she said.

"Very nasty." Em waved her hand in front of her face, helped

Tilda down, gave her an unnecessary clean up and righted her britches. "How do you feel now?"

Tilda put her hands on her middle, then said, "Hey! My tummy's all better!"

Emily felt almost weak with relief.

∼

Joe slammed the back door of the Long Branch when he entered, stalked through the kitchen and into the office and slammed its door as well. He felt his brothers' eyes on him as he passed through the gleaming kitchen, but he didn't acknowledge them.

He opened the desk drawer, took out a bottle of expensive Scotch whiskey and poured three fingers worth into a crystal glass.

The tap on the office door came before he even downed his first sip. He sipped anyway, then looked up to see his brothers looking at him.

He didn't invite them to come in. They came anyway.

"What's going on, Joe?" Jason asked, looking around the office that had once been mainly his, and had gradually become more and more Joey's.

Joe looked up, met Jason's eyes, then Rob's, then lowered his head and shook it slowly. "It's not for public consumption."

"We're not public. We're your brothers," Rob said. He came further in and pulled one of the chairs closer to the front of the antique wooden desk. "And we're not going tell anyone if you ask us not to. Maybe we can help."

"I don't need help."

"You're drinking before noon on a weekday." Jason perched on the edge of the desk. "You either need help or an intervention."

"I'm not drinking. I'm having a drink."

"Subtle distinction," Jason said.

"What did that girl do to you?" Rob asked.

Joey sighed heavily, opened the bottom drawer and fetched two more glasses from it. He set them on the desk and poured. Then he handed one to each brother, and lifted his glass.

Frowning at each other, his brothers picked up theirs.

"Congratulations," Joey said, lifting his glass a bit higher. "You're uncles."

Then he slugged back the entire contents and smacked the tumbler down onto the desk.

His brothers gaped at him, maybe still not getting it. "I'm a father," he said. Emily has a little girl with her. My little girl."

"Holy smokes," Rob said, and he downed his drink as well.

Joey would've smiled at that on any other day. It was something his pretty little Kiley was always saying, and Rob had picked up the habit.

"Wait, wait now." Jason set his glass down without so much as a sip. "She has a child with her?"

Joey nodded. "Matilda Louise," he said. Then something in him went soft, and his anger faded into the background. "She's three and a half, and she's the prettiest little thing this side of the Pecos. All big brown eyes and goldilocks curls." And then his anger returned. "I never would've believed Emily could do something as rotten as to keep a little girl from her daddy."

Rob got up from his chair, looking thunderstruck. "Did you ask her why?"

Joe shrugged. "Like there could be a good enough reason?"

"I can't imagine one," Rob said. "But you can't be sure until you ask her."

Jason said, "A better question is why she's changed her mind. Why is she here? Why now? What does she want?"

"You stormed out of there without even asking for an explanation, didn't you?" Rob asked.

"Tell me you didn't scare the kid." Jason was looking at him as if he thought that was a real possibility.

"Of course I didn't scare that sweet little angel," Joe said. "I held my temper so hard I think I broke something. But I'm not gonna take this sitting down, I'll tell you that."

"What are you gonna do?" Rob asked softly.

"I'd suggest getting proof she's yours, to begin with," Jason said. "Sophie can probably facilitate a DNA test for you. Once that's done, assuming she's yours, you need to find out what Emily wants. She keeps the baby a secret for three and a half years, and then she just shows up out of the blue to tell you about her? She's after something, Joe."

"Cynical much?" Rob asked.

"She's after something," Jason repeated.

"What are you gonna do?"

Joe reached for the bottle, but instead of pouring from it as he'd first intended, he put the cap back on. "I'm gonna take her to see Santa Claus this afternoon. In between, I think I'll go pay Caleb a visit."

"You might not need a lawyer, Joe," Rob said. "Why don't you talk to Emily first? Maybe there are factors you don't know—"

"Talk to Caleb," Jason said. "At least you'll know what your options are."

Joe nodded. "This doesn't go any further. Not until I'm ready. I don't need the whole fam-damily meddling in my business. They'll send Emily running scared."

The boys nodded. Jason clapped him on the shoulder. "We're here for you, Joe."

Rob nodded hard. "Whatever you need, man. Just say the word."

Joey believed them. His brothers were his best friends. They'd always have his back, and he'd always have theirs. He met their concerned eyes, and then smiled a little crookedly.

"Wait till you see her," he said. "She's smart as a whip, and pretty as a daisy."

"I'll bet she is," Rob said.

"Who'd have thought little Joe would be the first of us to become a daddy?" Jason asked.

"Not me, that's for damn sure." The phone started ringing. Jason said, "I'll get it. Take some time, Joe. I've got the place for today. All right?"

Nodding, Joey got up and left them in the office. He walked through the saloon, to the wide staircase that spilled into it, and then up to the second floor and into his room up there. It was just a guest room, small with an attached bathroom, but he'd had great plans. The drawings were taped to his wall. He'd planned to convert the entire second story into living space, sprawling, spacious and as opulent as the upstairs of a saloon could get. He was the son of a billionaire, one of the two most eligible bachelors in Big Falls, and he'd intended to live up to that.

Now, he didn't know what the hell he wanted.

There were also drawings of his plans for the outdoor additions to the Long Branch. Dodge City Shootout, a paintball range with bad guys and innocent bystanders that popped up randomly. A stagecoach-playhouse you could climb all over. A Cherokee themed mini-golf course.

He could imagine Matilda Louise playing on all of it, and him carrying her around on his shoulders, keeping her safe, playing with her, teaching her.

She didn't even know he was her daddy. Would he be within his rights to tell her? He didn't need Emily's permission or approval to do that, did he? The poor little thing ought to know she had a father. Or had Emily cast some other man in that role? Was his little girl calling another man Daddy?

Sighing heavily, he put his hat back on and headed out to talk to his cousin-in-law, the lawyer.

Hours later, Joey sat in a booth near the front of the Big Falls Diner. His very new sister-in-law Kiley, sat across from him. She had cocoa. The chocolate mustache on her upper lip went really well with the freckles across the bridge of her nose.

Emily and his little girl hadn't arrived yet and he was getting antsy, looking every few seconds at the door, then at the big old schoolroom style clock on the wall above it. It was only five of. He shouldn't be nervous yet. But he couldn't stop worrying that she might just up and leave for parts unknown, taking that sweet little girl with him and robbing Joe of even more time with her.

"So this Emily Hawkins," Kiley said, interrupting his thoughts. "Old flame?"

He shifted his attention back to her. He liked her, had from the start, even when she was a con artist. "Worse yet. First love," he said.

"She break your heart, Joey?"

"She did. Turns out it was a narrow escape though. She's not the girl I thought she was."

The door jangled, and when it opened a flash flood of noise swept right through it. His stepsisters Maya and Kara and their kids came right along with it. Tyler was pretty quiet, but then he was eleven now. The twins, Cal and Dahlia, one on each side of their mamma, were bouncing up and down and talking at once.

"I wanted to go to Sunny's! I want a half-moon cookie!"

"I want pie! Aunt Rosie's has the best pie!"

Rosie, who managed the place—though most people thought she owned it—cut loose a whistle, and when they went silent and fixed their wide little eyes on her, she said, "I have half-moons from Sunny's right here in the case, Dahlia."

"You do?" Dahlia asked.

"What, you think I bake all this stuff myself?"

The two moms sent her grateful looks and proceeded to order, a process he knew, from experience would take a full five minutes as each child asked questions and changed choices.

"What did she do to you, Joey?"

Kiley pulled his attention back to their conversation. "You'll find out soon enough. I might need a day or so." She was too curious, and he knew better than to think she'd let it drop. Time for a new topic. "How are you, anyway? Have you heard from your father or sister since they skipped town?"

She took a long breath, averted her eyes. "Kendra says Dad figured out what I'd done before they'd gone ten miles. Wanted to come back right then, but she talked him out of it."

"Come back and do what?" he asked, suddenly concerned. Kiley's dad was fresh out of prison. He'd swindled the town out of a fortune, and Kiley had managed to swindle it right back. There was no telling what the man might be capable of.

She shrugged. "Doesn't matter. Kendra will let me know if I need to worry."

"And you'll let us know."

She nodded hard, then performed an adept topic change of her own. "You remember Dax? How he helped us out with that whole thing?"

"I remember him better by how he beat the crap outta my brother."

She waved a dismissive hand, "Shoot, Rob's over that. They're friends now." She sighed. "I think he's in trouble."

Joey not only remembered Dax. He was a hard guy not to like. Big and kind of goofy from time to time. Sweet natured enough to have been conned by Kiley's twin sister, and then still step up to help them both out of a fix all the same. "In trouble how?"

"He's drinking, Joe. A lot."

A good woman could make a man's world. A bad one could do just the opposite. And Kiley's sister Kendra Kellogg was a bad woman. "I'll check up on him. You know where he's staying?"

"Tucker Lake Hotel, but I'd like him here, where I can keep an eye on him. He's been helping Rob with the horses a few days a week, but lately…he's just stopped showing up."

"I'll check on him."

Kiley lifted her brows. "You will?"

"Of course I will. If you want, I'll even go fetch him back here, tuck him in one of the rooms upstairs. Haven't started remodeling the place yet anyway. And hell, I need help around the Long Branch like nobody's business." He shrugged. "Besides, you're family. Your friends are my friends."

Maya, Kara, and the kids came to the table, but walked right on past. "Restroom," Kara shout-whispered. They moved through the place like a herd of bison.

The door jangled again, and he and Kiley both looked up at once.

And then his breath got caught in his throat, just like it always had when Emily stepped into his line of sight. She was as beautiful as ever. Her hair was a mingling of tones from copper to gold, and crazy curly. He could imagine her running wild in some Scottish moor in days gone by. She met his eyes, and hers were guarded, wary. She gave a nod.

"Can I get one of those, Mommy?"

He looked down at Matilda standing by her side, holding her hand, and pointing at the half-moon cookie Rosie was pulling from the case.

"Ho*leee* smokes," Kiley whispered.

"You can have anything you want, Matilda Louise," Joey said, clasping the envelope on the seat beside him, and sliding out of his booth. "You're hanging out with me today." He went to the counter and handed the envelope to Emily. Her eyes widened and snapped to his.

"What is this?"

He thinned his lips and shifted his gaze to Matilda. And then he forgot to be angry. He melted every time he looked at her. She was standing on tiptoe to accept the big, tissue-wrapped half-moon cookie Rosie was handing down to her and smiling big enough to light a small city.

"That's enough sugar to put a horse into overdrive," Emily said.

Rosie laughed softly. "We'll get the whole crew tanked up for their visit with Santa," Rosie said, sending Joey a wink. "After all, it's Uncle Joey's problem now, isn't it kids?"

She looked toward the back, and he turned to see that the crew had come out of the restroom. The kids came running at him yelling "Uncle Joey!" all at once, and then they were all wrapped around every appendage, hanging on and giggling.

His stepsisters were looking from him to Matilda Louise and back again, and their eyes were as big as his little princess's had been when they'd first spotted that cookie.

"Holeeeeeee smokes," Kiley said again.

Hell. She knew.

"Who's those kids, Uncle Joey?" Tilda asked. She stood a little apart from them, her cookie in a two-handed grip with a big bite out of the top, her mouth already frosting-coated.

It brought a lump to his throat to hear her call him that. Yeah, he knew she was just imitating his actual niece and nephews. But he wasn't her uncle, dammit. He was her daddy. And he told Emily so with a swift look he hoped was unmistakable.

But then he pushed all that aside, and opened his arm wider to rest it around Tilda's shoulders, very lightly. She snuggled right into the group hug, so he guessed it was all right, and then he straightened. "This big guy is Tyler," he said, cupping Ty's head with his palm. "He's eleven years old. And this guy," he cupped Cal's much smaller noggin, "is Cal and he's gonna turn five on Christmas Eve. And this gorgeous little girl is his twin sister, Dahlia, same exact age." He stroked

Dahlia's pretty hair, and gave her nose a tweak, making her giggle.

"Kids, this is Matilda Louise."

"You can call me Tilda," she said, twisting her hands in front of her and moving her upper body side to side.

"Tilda's gonna come with us to see Santa."

"Cool!" Tyler said. "Hi there, Tilda."

"How old are you?" Dahlia asked.

"Three and a half. So midas well say four."

He smiled at the mixed up words, then glanced up at Em, who seemed to be seething, and his joy died a little. "Emily Hawkins, these are my sisters, Maya and Kara, and you've already met my sister-in-law Kiley." He nodded toward each woman as he spoke and considered his duty done. "You kids ready?"

"Sisters?" Emily said. He was ignoring her, and she put a hand on his shoulder to get his attention. "Stepsisters or half?"

"Sisters," he said. "I don't qualify it. They're family. Try to be nice to them. Come on kids, take your treats to go and let's get in line before it's around the block."

∼

Emily was in enemy territory and she knew it. She watched the kids march past the counter, each taking his or her treat from the woman behind it, and heading for the door with Joey leading the way like some kind of cowboy pied piper.

She lifted her head, looking toward the three women who were still standing near the back, still looking kind of stunned.

The taller of the two beautiful brunettes said, "Stepsisters. Selene's his half sister. Nice to meet you, Emily. Sorry Joey's manners aren't better. He tends to forget the rest of us when he's with the kids. Why don't you come join us?"

The redheaded waitress—or maybe owner—came out from

behind the counter with a big tray full of coffee and pastries, pausing behind Em and whispering. "Courage, now. They're good women. Best I know." She brought her head level again, beamed a bright smile, and carried the tray to the table as the two brunettes slid into the booth facing the front and the strawberry blonde on the side facing the back.

Emily stiffened her spine and went to join them. She'd seen their eyes, the way they'd been looking at Tilda and Joey. They saw the resemblance. She'd wondered if Tilda really looked as much like her father as she'd always thought, or if it was just her imagination. Now she knew.

When she reached the table, a polite smile plastered on her face, she remained standing. Rosie set the mugs on the table, added a large pot, and dropped platter of assorted cookies and brownies in the middle. "Let me know if you need anything else."

"You have any jeans back there bigger than the ones I'm wearing?" Maya asked. "Cause I'm clearly not gonna fit these by the time I leave here."

Rosie winked and headed back to her station.

Kiley patted the bench beside her. "Come on, we can't eat all these cookies ourselves."

"Okay, but um, Maya, is it?" she asked the one on the outside of the front-facing side of the booth. "Would you mind letting me sit there?"

"Of course not." Maya got up, grabbed her bag from the seat, and moved around to sit beside Kiley on the other side.

"Thanks." Emily slid in beside Kara and immediately scanned the line of kids across the street. There was a circular town park that bisected Main Street, with a giant, decked-out Christmas tree at its center. Santa Claus sat on a red velvet upholstered throne in a tooled wooden pavilion suitable for a Hindu God.

She spotted Tilda right away, bouncing and fidgeting with

the three other kids who surrounded Joey. He stood taller than most of the parents in the line and was talking and laughing with the kids. He seemed as excited as they were.

She didn't understand any of this. His reactions made no sense.

"So, does Joey know she's his?" Kiley asked.

Emily looked at her quickly, then at the others.

Kara whispered, "*Kiley.*"

Maya pinched the bridged of her nose and closed her eyes.

"Well? We all saw it, didn't we? We gonna pretend we didn't? She's like his tiny female mini-me."

"I'm sorry, Emily," Kara said. "You don't have to tell us anything if you don't want to."

"I don't want to," she replied. And maybe it was a little bit rude, but it was enough already.

Everyone nodded. Kiley snatched a cookie off the plate and bit into it like she was ripping off its head.

"So Emily, how do you know Joey?" Maya asked.

If she wasn't mistaken, Maya was the oldest. What she didn't know was whether this was an attempt at small talk or the beginning of an interrogation.

"My father worked for his father back in Texas," she said. "We kind of grew up together."

"You *have* known him a long time," Maya said.

"All our lives." Em shifted her gaze to the window again. The kids were already at the front of the line. Santa's lap was vacated, and they all rushed forward. Joey said something, and they stopped, and then he crouched and picked up Tilda. He held her up high and spun her around as she giggled, and then lowered her right down onto Santa's knee.

Had she done a terrible thing, Emily wondered?

No. *He* had. He'd tried to pay her to abort their child, that very child he was gazing at with tears welling in his eyes.

"Littlest first," Kara said, leaning across the table. "Tyler hates that rule, being the oldest of his generation."

"And Dahlia loves it, because her brother was born a few minutes before her," Maya said.

Kiley stuck out her tongue. "That rule needs to be abolished. Make 'em play rock, paper, scissors or something."

"You were the firstborn twin, weren't you Kiley?" Kara handed her another cookie. "Here. For your suffering."

"Thank you."

Emily looked back outside. Tilda was finished with Santa, and Joey was lifting her down. He set her on her feet beside him and reached for Dahlia, who shook her head, and went to climb onto Santa's knee all by herself, thank-you-very-much.

"They really are okay with him, you know," Maya said.

"The kids love him," Kara said.

"We love him, too," Kiley added. And Emily thought there might be a hint of a threat under the words.

Emily nodded, meeting their eyes, and then clasping her mug, she picked it up and slid out of the booth. "I'm gonna get some air. It's a little close in here." She headed for the door, pausing at the counter. "What do I owe?" she asked.

"Joey took care of it."

"I'll pay for my own. And for my little girl's cookie, too. How much?"

Frowning, the woman punched keys on the register.

While Em was waiting for her change, Maya came up to her and spoke softly. "The envelope he gave you has my husband's logo on it. Just so you know what to expect."

"What's your husband do?" Emily asked.

"He's a lawyer."

CHAPTER FOUR

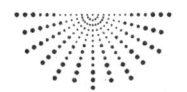

As he watched his little girl—his little girl. He couldn't get over it—whispering her wishes into Santa Claus's ear, Joey's chest felt so swollen, he thought it was liable to burst.

"She's so cute," Tyler whispered, leaning up.

He was growing up fast. Too fast. A rush of hot anger followed the thought, anger at being denied three whole years and seven months of Tilda's life, time he could never get back.

Then Tilda was looking his way, so he had to get her down. And he realized as he reached for her that his anger was gone. Just looking at her zapped it like lightning zapping a sinner, as his stepmother Vidalia would say.

Tilda widened her eyes and shouted WAIT! like someone was about to get hit by a bus. "I almost forgot, Santa. You gotta get Mommy somethin' to make her happy. She's very sad and I don't know why."

Santa Claus sent Joey a look, and he could've sworn his eyes twinkled. Then he smiled, and slapped his opposite knee, and ho-ho-ho'd in a way that seemed entirely natural to him. "Don't you worry, little Tilda. Santa's on the job."

"I love you, Santa Claus," she said, and leaned up to kiss him on his bearded cheek. Then she swung around and reached for Joey.

He scooped her up and set her on her feet, then reached for Dahlia, who was almost five and didn't want his help. She told Santa that she wanted a puppy, and everything else could be a surprise, because she loved surprises.

Then it was Cal's turn.

Cal had a whole list of things to tell Santa. But most of all, he wanted a horse, not a pony, but a horse. It would be no problem at all, he explained fervently. It could live at his uncle Robby's ranch, and he would personally go over there to take care of it before and after school. He was sure this would be okay with his uncle.

Tyler lingered beside Joey for a beat longer than he needed to after he helped Cal down.

An "elf" was handing out candy canes, distracting the kids, so he hunkered down to eye level with him. "What's the matter, Ty?"

The boy pressed the toe of one shoe into the ground. "I don't know. Some of the kids in my class don't believe any more, but..."

"But...?"

He shrugged.

"Yeah, sometimes I have trouble with it, too," Joey said. "But I figure either he's for real, or he's not. Now, if he's not, and I believe he is, no harm done, right? But if he *is*, oh boy if he is, and I believe he's not...I'm missing out."

Tyler looked at him with his mouth open. "Wow. I never thought'a that."

"See? I'm just saying. Might as well cover all your bases, you know?"

He nodded hard. "I asked him for a mom when me and Dad first came out here. And then Dad married Kara. Right at Christmastime!" He blinked. "I got the puppy I asked for, too!"

"Seems to me you just answered your own question. You don't need to admit anything to the guys in school. The way I look at it, it's between you and the big guy right there."

Tyler smiled, looked very much relieved and went right up to Santa. "Is it okay if I don't sit on your lap?"

"You can sit on my footstool, Tyler," Santa Claus said, pulling it closer.

Tyler sat down. Joey was gathering Dahlia and Cal and sweet little Tilda into a closer huddle, and unwrapped their candy canes for them.

"You're the same Santa from last year," Tyler said.

"I'm the same Santa from *every* year."

He was. Joey remembered him. His name was Nick and he was only seen around town in the winter. Kept to himself, had a cabin in the woods up behind the falls. His stints as the Big Falls Santa were the only socializing he seemed to do.

"Can I pull your beard?" Tyler asked.

"You asked me that last year," Santa said. But he extended his chin. "Not too hard now."

Tyler tugged, then nodded. "I want my own cell phone and a gift card for more apps, and I want *Death Squad Four* for my PlayStation. I should say I want Mom and Dad to let me *have* Death Squad Four for my PlayStation. And a four wheeler."

"A four wheeler!" Santa gasped. "Oh, four wheelers are strictly parental requests, my boy. But I think I can help you out with the rest."

"Thanks. Santa."

"You're welcome, Tyler. How's the puppy? What'd you name him again? Red?"

Tyler widened his eyes as he got down. Even Joey wondered how the old man knew such a personal detail. "He's awesome," Ty said. "He's all grown up now. I think he's the best dog ever."

Joe nodded, extremely satisfied with the way the visit had gone. "Thank you, Santa. Merry Christmas."

"You're welcome, Joe." Nick stretched out his hand to shake, and when Joey clasped it, he passed him a note.

He frowned, but pocketed it to look at later. Probably a coupon from a toy store or something. Then he gathered all the children and headed back through the park. They stopped to look at the Christmas tree and listened to some carolers, and then he figured he should deliver them all back to their waiting mothers, though he really wasn't ready to surrender Matilda.

He looked down at her walking beside him, and she reached up her arms, so he scooped her right up and she giggled. And in spite of himself, he said, "Why do you think your mamma's sad, Tilda?"

"She cries sometimes." She said it very seriously.

He frowned, a little bit of guilt creeping over his conscience like a spreading black mold. "Did you ever ask her what's wrong, when she's crying?"

"I just snuggle. Mommy *loves* snuggles."

Maybe he'd jumped the gun a little with his visit to Caleb. Maybe serving Emily with a court order wasn't the best opening move.

Maybe she'd come here because she was in some kind of trouble. Maybe he should have asked her.

He returned to the diner. Emily was standing just outside the front door, under the green and white striped awning in front of the big front window with BIG FALLS DINER painted on it in country-style lettering, and fake snow sprayed strategically on the glass.

Emily took Tilda from him, transferring her easily from his hip to her own and anchoring an arm around her. "Did you talk to Santa?" she asked. Her entire focus was on the little girl. She didn't so much as spare Joey a glance.

Tilda nodded. "He's the real one, Mommy."

"What did you ask him for?"

"That's personal."

Joey laughed. Then he caught Emily's hateful glare and flinched a little. She lowered one hand to her bag, took hold of the envelope he'd given her, and said, "You couldn't even give it a day, could you?"

He pressed his lips. "We should get together and talk," he said. "After you read the papers, I mean."

"I was planning on it. You didn't need to do this."

Then she turned and carried Tilda away from the diner, down the sidewalk to where the van was parked. She hit a button and the door slid opened. He stood there like an idiot, watching as she buckled the little girl into her car seat, then hit the button again and got behind the wheel.

As the side door slid slowly closed, Tilda met his eyes, grinned big, and waved her little chubby hand at him. His heart melted. Her mother glared.

Well, he might not have handled this whole thing in exactly the best way. But whatever he did, Emily had it coming. Keeping that little girl from him. It burned his insides every time he thought of it.

He shoved his hands into his coat pockets and felt Nick's note, pulled it out and gave it a read.

For Tyler, Death Squad Four *is releasing a version with parental controls on the 15th. It's a digital download. You can pre-order. Tilda wants a baby that looks and feels like a real one, and a firetruck pedal car with a real siren. They don't make one with a siren, so get busy. Also, don't worry. It's going to be okay. Merry Christmas.*

—Nick

Emily backed her van up, turned and drove away. He watched her go, then heard the bell on the diner's door jingle, and was immediately surrounded by women. Maya and Kara had their hands full, but they each gave him a hug, made their children thank him, and then they headed away. Kiley stood there, staring at him with two white paper bags in one hand and a foam mug in the other.

She held up the two bags. "Take the one in front. It's for you."

"Cookies? From Sunny's Place?" He took the bag then opened it up to peer inside to find his guess was right.

"Walk me to the Jeep," Kiley said.

"Sure." He reached for the coffee in her other hand, and she danced it out of reach. "Uh-uh. No way, this is mine."

He grinned. "Don't bite my hand off."

She heaved a sigh. "So?"

He looked at her. "What?"

"Uh, hello? She looks just like you, Joey. Everybody saw it. That's your little girl." Then she blinked. "You do know that, right?"

He paused a beat, then nodded. "Yeah, as of earlier today."

"Holy...really?" Then she frowned. "That *bitch*."

"Yeah, well...maybe she had a reason."

"What, she hasn't told you why yet?"

"I don't think I really gave her the chance to." He swallowed hard as they arrived at her little red Wrangler. She handed him her coffee, then opened the door and got in, setting her purse and bag of cookies on the passenger seat, buckling her seatbelt, all while he stood there.

Then she took the cup back, took a sip, and set it into the cup holder. "You're gonna have to tell the family. This isn't gonna stay a secret very long."

"Maybe a day," he said.

"More like an hour." A text tone came from her purse, and she glanced its way and held up one finger. "Four, three, two..." It chimed again. And then again. And then two more chimes came in quick succession. "Nope. Not even an hour. I'm gonna play dumb, Joey, but uh, you're gonna need to talk to your family."

"I think I need to talk to Emily first."

"Might've been a good idea to do that before you served her with whatever those papers from Caleb's office were."

"Maybe."

"Does Matilda know?" she asked. "That you're her dad?"

He shook his head slowly. "I want her to know."

She nodded again. "Talk to Emily, Joe."

"I will."

She closed the Jeep door. Joey looked back the way Emily had gone. She was angry. And he couldn't really blame her.

But he was angrier. She'd done far worse to him than serve him with legal papers. She'd stolen more than three years of his daughter's life from him. He didn't think that was something he would ever be able to forgive.

∽

Emily and Matilda Louise stood holding hands and staring up at the town Christmas tree. "We should see it at nighttime," Em said softly. She was trying real hard to put aside her anger at Joey. Those papers had been a court order, forbidding her from taking Tilda out of this godforsaken town until there was a hearing to determine his parental rights.

She'd snapped pics of each page, emailed the whole thing to her lawyer in New Mexico, and told herself to put it out of her mind. It didn't matter. He'd realize that, too, once she told him what she had to tell him this morning. "As pretty as the tree is now, it'll be even prettier in the dark," she told her little girl.

"Why?" Tilda didn't look her way. She was busy admiring the ornaments on the towering evergreen.

"Because the lights show up better in the dark."

Tilda swung her head up, eyes wide. "Can we get a tree that big?"

"Our house isn't big enough for a tree that big, honey."

She pouted. Then blinked and said, "We need a bigger house."

"It would almost have to be a castle to fit a tree that big," a woman said.

She had been admiring the tree too from a nearby park bench, but now she was standing beside them, smiling down at Matilda with eyes that just about sparkled.

She might've been forty, or she might've been fifty, or maybe even sixty. She had long wavy hair, mostly black but with strands of silver decorating it like holiday tinsel, a kind face, beautiful brown eyes.

"You must be Emily. I've heard wonderful things about you," she said, smiling, and then crouching lower and extending a hand, said, "And you must be Matilda. I'm so happy to meet you."

"Nice to meet you, too," Matilda said giving the stranger a very grown up handshake.

Emily's alarm bells were going off. "And you are?"

Rising, smiling, she said, "I'm Vidalia Brand McIntyre, Bobby Joe's wife." She smiled even bigger, refocusing on Tilda. "I'm Dahlia and Cal and Tyler's grandma."

"Wow," Tilda said. "I don't have any grandmas."

The woman blinked so fast Emily knew there must be tears threatening. She expected something then, a hateful look or at least an accusing one, but none manifested. Instead, the woman looked at her with kindness, and said, "You two are so very welcome here. I'm just overjoyed that you came to Big Falls for Christmas. It's like Santa brought my present early."

Em wasn't sure how to react to that. "That's...nice of you to say."

"It's sincere," she said. "Anything you need, Emily, anything at all, you call me, you hear? You're among family here. We've got your back."

"Morning, ladies." Joey had come up behind them.

Em turned quickly. A little jolt shot through her every time she saw him or heard his voice. It touched some nerve in her auditory canal and sparked like a rock striking flint.

"Morning, Uncle Joey." Tilda opened her arms.

Joe dropped down on one knee and opened his, and she ran right into them. Emily's heart cramped up, but she reminded herself that Tilda was at that age where anything was everything. A single M&M was ecstasy to her. A hug. A pretty Christmas tree in a town park. A grandma. A handsome man who paid her special attention.

Her father.

"Hello, Joey," Vidalia said. "I'd like a word with you later." It sounded vaguely threatening, and her eyes said he might be in trouble.

Emily wondered why. Vidalia obviously knew he had a daughter, but he hadn't known himself, so she couldn't be upset that he hadn't told her. The court order, maybe? Her daughters knew about that. They'd probably told her. But it didn't seem likely.

"I have to run," Vidalia went on, her face friendly and kind again. "It was such a treat meeting you, ladies. I hope we see a lot of each other while you're in town." Turning, she added, "Be sure she has my number, Joseph."

"I will." Joe straightened up to his full height with Tilda in one arm.

He either didn't notice that Emily hadn't yet spoken to him, or didn't care.

"I want a tree that big," Tilda told him, pointing at the town tree. "But Dahlia's gramma says we'd need a castle."

"Well one of these days, maybe you'll live in a castle."

"Really?"

"Anything is possible, Tilda. Especially when you're still a kid."

She smiled, her face close to his, and poked his nose with her forefinger.

"Big houses aren't important, though, right Tilda?" Emily said.

Joey's gaze was on her, but she didn't meet it.

"What's important is being a good person. Right?"

Tilda looked at her, frowning, her lips pressed into a pink rosebud. "But, Mommy, can't good people have giant Christmas trees?"

"Or live in castles or great big houses?" Joey added.

Emily looked at him, caught in her own bad behavior. Using her child to scold him for his values. That was wrong. She deserved it. "Of course they can," she said. No choice, she wasn't going to lie to her baby.

Joey had a white paper bag in his free hand, and he held it up. "I got takeout from Sunny's. There's coffee in the truck. Cocoa for you, Peanut." He poked her nose like she'd poked his, and she giggled.

And his face, my God, it split in a grin as big as all outdoors. He was beautiful when he smiled. "We um...we'll need the car seat, she's still—"

"I've got one already." He carried Tilda toward his truck, parked diagonally in one of the painted spaces that lined Main Street on both sides of the park. He opened the door. It hadn't been locked. As he tucked Tilda into a flowery pink car seat and began pulling out and examining straps and buckles, he said, "I borrowed this one from my sister Maya. It was Dahlia's. But I'm gonna get a much better one. We'll find one that matches the truck."

"Trucks aren't ideal, though," Emily said, her nerves as jittery as they always were when anyone else was closer to her child than she was. Doctor's appointments drove her to the brink of insanity. She was going to have to get used to them, though. "Kids are safer in the back seat—"

"Because of air bags," he said. "I researched it last night. There's no center airbag in this truck."

"She could go through the windshield," she whispered behind him, quietly enough that Tilda wouldn't hear and get scared.

"Not if I can figure these straps out," he said, glancing at Tilda, not back at Em. "It's like a spider's web."

Emily started to reach around him. "I can—"

He moved to block her hand's path. "I've got this," he said, pulling the straps in front of Tilda's shoulders, gently moving her arms through them. They were adjusted pretty close to perfectly already, so he snapped them into place and nodded in satisfaction. Then he moved out of the way so Emily could get in. She climbed up and wondered why he didn't install a rope ladder on the running boards. He was walking around the front of the truck, and she quickly bent to tug on each of the car seat's buckles, making sure they were secure.

He'd seen her though. Too bad. He got in and started the engine.

"Where are we going?" Emily asked. She'd texted him last night to set up this early-morning meeting and discuss his stupid court order. And to tell him why she'd brought Matilda here.

"Kara's place," he said. "She offered to keep an eye on Tilda so we can talk." He kept his eyes on the road, not looking her way at all.

She sat there, fuming and stunned right to her toes.

He glanced sideways, just a quick look. "What?" he asked.

It took her a couple of tries to form words. She forced herself not to shout them. "I'm not in the habit of leaving my little girl with people I don't know," she said.

He opened his mouth, closed it again, looked sideways at her, then down at Tilda, and quickly back to the road again. "Maybe you can decide when we get there." He turned onto a side road that looped up a hill and back around in the direction they'd come from. Neat homes lined it, with plenty of distance in between. And they pulled over in front of the neatest one of all. A two story farmhouse with fresh white paint, and a pretty door with an oval stained glass window from top to bottom. Then he opened his door and got out, reaching back to unfasten Tilda's buckles.

"Joey, you can't just—"

"We're here. We might as well go in and say hello." He looked around Matilda at her. "That's all. I won't go against your wishes. Okay?"

It irked him to say that. She could see it. God, he was going to be a problem. She had not expected him to act like he had rights to Tilda.

But he did. He did have rights. And it was making her crazy.

She unbuckled and got out, jumping to the ground, a distance of about three stories. A female voice called, "Come around back!" and Joey headed over the paved driveway around the house to the rear.

Emily followed, then stood there blinking. There was a beautiful wooden fence with a gate fit for a fairytale, surrounding a playground from a child's fantasy. A huge sandbox, a climbing gym, several twisty slides, none of them scary high, a swing set, and a half dozen pedal cars were inside that fence. Matilda loved pedal cars. There was a foot-deep bed of rubber mulch under anything a kid could fall from, and neatly trimmed grass everywhere else. A concrete path twisted around the outermost edge like a miniature racetrack, presumably for the pedal cars. There were six toddlers playing happily, a reddish mixed-breed dog dancing around the kids, and a boy who could've been a teen idol, apparently helping to wrangle them.

"Morning, Joey!" Kara said, coming to the gate and opening it to let them in. "Morning Emily."

"M-morning."

Kara was already crouching down to Tilda's eye level. "Good morning, Tilda. Would you like to come and play?"

"Yeah!" Tilda looked up at her mother. "Can I?"

"Sure you can, honey."

And she ran right inside, going up to another little girl and striking up a conversation.

"She'll be fine here if you want to leave her for a little bit," Kara said. "We'll be outside for an hour. Oh, by the way, that's Max. Sophie and Darryl's boy."

"Sophie…as in the town doctor?" Em asked.

Kara nodded. "The one and only. Max is a fantastic young man. He's almost as great with kids as Joey is. He works for me part time."

Joey looked at Emily. She felt put on the spot, but she also felt like an overprotective idiot. The kids in Kara's yard were clean and happy and perfectly safe. The dog was clearly no threat. It seemed almost to be watching over the children. Kara obviously ran a daycare out of her home, and by all appearances, it was a good one.

"We can just walk out to the ball field and back," Joey said, pointing beyond the back yard. In the distance, she could see a sports field and realized the school was only up the street another house or two.

She glanced again at the play yard, then nodded. "Okay."

"Great." Joey ran back to the truck, reached in, and returned with a giant paper bag from Sunny's. "I brought enough donuts to share," he said. "Tilda hasn't had breakfast yet. There's cocoa in the truck. Wait."

Kara took the bag in two fingers and grimaced. "Yeah, um how about I start her off with a homemade oatmeal raisin bar and some juice? We can save the sugar for later." She looked at Emily and winked. "Men. Am I right?"

Emily's spine relaxed a little bit. "Thanks for keeping her."

Tilda was already deeply involved with three other children in an apparent sandbox road construction project.

"Tilda? Mamma and Joey are going to walk out there and back," she said, pointing toward the ball field. Tilda glanced up at her, looked where she was pointing, then went right back to pushing sand with a toy bulldozer. "You'll be able to see us the whole time. Okay?"

Nothing.

"Tilda?"

"What?"

"Will you be okay?"

Tilda grinned. "Anything's popsicle when you're a kid!"

Almost automatically, she looked at Joey. He was grinning as much as she was. Their eyes met, and there was this moment of absolute unity. This moment of two proud parents beaming over the cute and clever thing their little girl had just said.

It felt good.

But it only lasted for a second, and then it faded, and they were enemies again.

∼

Joey walked slowly past the play yard into the deep grass-and-wildflower strewn meadow between Kara's place and the well-mown school property. "She's safe with Kara," he said. It was a little insulting the way Emily couldn't stop looking back. "I wouldn't have left her there if she wasn't."

"Yeah, well, you might feel secure, but I just met the woman yesterday."

"*The woman* is my sister."

"Stepsister."

"Sister." He didn't remember her being this ornery. And her overprotectiveness! By God it was lucky he'd found out about Tilda when he had. Her mother would turn her into a nervous wreck. She'd grow up afraid of her own shadow if it was left up to Em.

They walked a few more steps. She said, "If you'd told me she ran a day care I wouldn't have been so—"

"Mean?"

She blinked at him. "I wasn't being mean. I was..." She lowered her head. "Never mind. What you think of me really doesn't have anything to do with anything. That's not what we need to talk about."

"The papers," he said. He stopped walking, swallowed his pride, turned to face her. "I've already been read the riot act about that."

"By whom?"

"Pretty much the entire family. And Vidalia's next in line and will probably try to bring a switch to the discussion." He sighed. "I told them about Tilda last night. That's why Vidalia showed up in the park this morning. She already considers Tilda her newest grandbaby, and I gotta tell you, that woman loves her grandbabies."

She closed her eyes as if that news was unexpected or something. Didn't she think he'd tell his family that he had a daughter, that they had a granddaughter, a niece, a cousin? Even if they hadn't all already known. But they had. One glance at Matilda and their family text loop had probably been using up every drop of bandwidth in town. He dragged himself back on topic. "I was angry. That was wrong, serving you with a court order without even talking to you first. I don't blame you for being mad about that."

She blinked in surprise. And then, frowning at him, said, "Then you'll drop it?"

He lifted his head fast. "Hell, no, I'm not gonna drop it. If I do, what's to stop you from taking Tilda and running for the hills with her? It's clear as day you don't want me having anything to do with her. I'm not gonna stand for it, Em. I'm sorry if that upsets you, but I'm her father."

She stared up at him, opened her mouth, closed it again. "This isn't the time to argue about this."

"Be reasonable and we won't have to argue at all. Look, Em, I don't want to take her away from you. She loves you, it would crush her little soul."

Tipping her head to one side, she said, "Then what *do* you want?"

"I want to get to know her," he said, keeping his voice calm, careful. "I want to be able to spend time with her."

She felt panic trying to take hold. "You have that right. I won't deny it. It's just...it's hard for me."

"And I want her to know who I am. That I'm her daddy."

"No." She blurted it so fast, he knew it had been an impulsive reaction.

"I'm afraid that's not negotiable, Emily. I'm her father. She has a right to know, and I have a right to tell her. You've stood between us long enough."

"I can't even believe you have the nerve to—"

"If you didn't want me in her life, then why the hell did you bring her here? Why did you even tell me about her?"

"Because she's sick!"

She could have punched him square in the nose and not hit him as hard as those words did.

"She's sick, Joey."

"I don't..." He looked back toward Kara's place. "She seems fine."

"I know she does."

"Well...what is it, what's wrong?"

"It's a rare blood disorder. Her body isn't producing enough red cells. She needs—"

"A bone marrow transplant," he said. His legs had turned to jelly. He looked around, spotted a wooden picnic table off in the brush where someone had either left it or dragged it, and headed for it. Sinking onto its bench, he whispered, "God, Em, tell me it's not Sanguis Morbo."

"How...how did you know?"

It was. God, it was. "My father had the same thing. She must've inherited it." He blinked, looking up at her. "They said it's always terminal, unless—"

"Unless we can find a match," she said. She came closer, sat down on the bench beside him.

"That's why you came."

She nodded. He couldn't stop looking at her, and suddenly the pain he'd glimpsed behind her eyes showed itself in its full form. Emily was devastated, terrified, heartbroken, and determined. And he'd served her with papers her first day in town.

"I thought you or someone in your family would be our best chance to find a match. You having a half sister is a bonus."

He nodded hard. "We'll all get tested. Sophie can get the wheels turning on that. You should set up an appointment as soon as—"

"I already did. We're seeing her later this morning."

As he looked at her, tears welled up in her eyes. And then they welled up in his own. He turned toward her, put his arms around her and pulled her close. She was stiff, almost pulling back from him a little. But then a sob wracked her entire body and she just collapsed against him and wept. It was wet and noisy and messy. He tightened his arms around her and held her, and tried not to cry like a baby. And then he cried anyway.

Eventually, his chest still heaving, he tried to pull it together. He straightened his body, looked at her face. Strands of her hair stuck to her tearstained cheeks.

"Rip it up," he said.

She blinked her eyes dry, searching his. "What—"

"The judge's order. Just tear it up. I'm sorry I did that to you. I didn't know."

Sniffling twice, she nodded. "You were angry."

"My anger doesn't mean crap right now." He got to his feet, straightened up his spine. "We're not gonna lose her, I'll tell you that much. It's good you brought her here. She's in the right place. Miracles happen in this place. It's...special."

"Miracles." She pressed her lips tight, spat the word. "I don't believe in miracles. Not anymore. I lost whatever faith I had in a pediatrician's office a few weeks ago when they told me...."

"We're not gonna lose our little girl," Joey said, and he said it as firmly and confidently as he could. "I promise you that. You can believe it. If it costs every dime my family has, we're gonna save her."

She stared at him, wide eyed, maybe surprised. He had no idea what she was thinking or feeling. But he thought he saw relief in her eyes. "The rest of this, visitation, all of that, it can wait. Let's get through this, first. We can fight over her later."

"So...truce, then?" she asked.

"Yeah. Truce."

She gave a staccato nod, pulled a pack of tissues from her pocket, wiped off her face. "How are we gonna hide our faces from her? She'll know we were crying."

"She's got her mamma's intellect, that's for sure."

She reached up to dab the moisture from his cheeks. "And her daddy's eyes."

She stared into them just for a minute, then looked away and started walking back. "Our appointment with Dr. Sophie's at ten," she said.

"I'll be ready."

"You...you're coming, too?"

He nodded. "She has two parents now, Em. You're not carrying this whole burden alone, not anymore."

CHAPTER FIVE

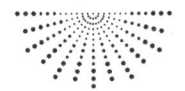

"I don't know how the hell I'm gonna hold it together, to be honest," Joe told his brothers a short while later.

He had dropped Emily and Tilda Lou back at Emily's van. She wanted to wash the play yard dirt off Tilda before her appointment with Sophie. And since they had another hour before that, he'd headed back to the Long Branch. His home.

He was a father and he lived in room above a saloon. Somehow it seemed completely ridiculous.

"But you *will* hold it together," Jason said, his voice an octave deeper since Joey had broken the news, his eyes as heavy as the weight of it.

"Yeah, you will," Rob agreed. "You don't really have a choice."

Joey nodded, knowing his brothers were right.

Jason and Rob had been there when Joey had returned, double checking the liquor order, they said. But he knew they were just eager to hear what he and Emily had talked about. They'd been with him last night when he'd got her text asking to meet. And so he'd told them, and even though they had yet to set eyes on Matilda Louise, the news had broken their big, strong hearts.

Sighing, he said, "I've got to hold onto hope, though. One of us will be a match. Or Dad or Selene."

"That's right," Rob said, nodding hard. "We thought we were gonna lose Dad, too, and look how that worked out."

"Vidalia says this town is a place with an abundance of miracles," Jason said. "I've never believed in that kind of thing, but it's hard to argue with the evidence."

Joey nodded. "I didn't believe in that kind of thing either, until we came here that Christmas we thought would be Dad's last. There's something about this Big Falls."

"Damn straight." Rob was looking at the gold band on his ring finger when he said it.

"What are you gonna do, Joe?" Jason asked.

"Figure out how to be a dad," he said.

"I meant the custody—"

"It can wait. Matilda's health takes priority over everything else. Not only that, but I need to spend every minute I can with her, in case…"

"We've got your back. We'll pitch in to run the place." Rob clapped him on the shoulder and went on. "And so will the rest of the family."

Jason nodded in solemn agreement.

He looked at his watch, then drained his root beer, which he figured was better than the real thing right before his kid's doctor's appointment. "I gotta go. Thanks guys."

They rose when he did, and Rob said, "What about the rest of the family? When are you gonna tell them?"

"It's the next thing on my list," he said. "Right after this appointment. You want to gather everybody together, right here?"

Jason looked at Rob. Rob nodded. "I'll activate the family emergency broadcast system."

"Who'd have thought that pain-in-the-ass group text function would ever come in handy?" Jason asked.

"Me. A coupla' times." Rob winked. "Noon, Joe?"

"Should be fine. Thanks, boys."

"Hang in there," Jason said, and he grabbed Joey in an uncharacteristic bear hug, and said it again. "Hang in there, little brother. We're gonna get through this together. As a family. And she may not know it yet, but that includes Emily."

"Yeah, whether she likes it or not." Rob clapped his arms around them to make it a group hug.

Joe felt himself getting all choked up again and wrestled himself free. "All right, all right, you guys are gonna have me bawling again. I can't show up at Sophie's place all teary eyed. Gotta be the man now."

"Gotta be the dad, now," Rob said, grinning. "I always thought you'd be the *last* McIntyre to produce an heir."

"You and me both," Joe replied. "See you at noon."

～

Emily had planned to meet Joey in the clinic's waiting room, but they never even paused there. The minute they'd walked through the stunning Victorian's massive hardwood front doors, a beautiful woman had greeted them with a stunning smile, and said, "You must be Emily. And Matilda! You're as pretty as my cousin Joey said you were." She crouched low. "I'm Dr. Sophie. But you can just call me Sophie, since we're family."

"We are?" Matilda asked.

Emily cleared her throat, drawing the blonde's gemstone eyes, which widened just a little. "Oh, right. Um, well, come on back with me. I've got a room all ready for you."

Then she led them to where they now waited, in a room painted pale blue with giraffes and alligators and monkeys frolicking on the walls. There was a little wooden desk and chair from days gone by, and Matilda sat there, making excellent use of the coloring books and crayons it held.

No one else had been in the clinic when they'd arrived. Emily found that odd and wondered why. But before she'd wondered long, the door opened, and Sophie came back in with Joey right behind her. Her eyes weren't quite as sparkling as before.

"Joey filled me in," she said. "As much as he could. I'll get more info from you, but first...." She brightened her expression and her voice as she turned to Tilda. "Would you mind terribly if I put you up on my table and took a look at you?"

Tilda set her crayon down, got to her feet and opened her arms to Joey. Not to Emily. It hurt like a knife in her heart.

But it seemed to have the opposite effect on him. He practically lit up as he obliged her unspoken request. He lifted her up high, and spun her around twice before lowering her carefully to the paper-covered exam table, while she giggled maniacally.

"Thank you, Joey," Sophie said, and she moved closer and proceeded to look into Tilda's eyes, ears, and down her throat with a light, to palpate her glands and her abdomen, to listen to her breathing and her heartbeat, to measure her blood pressure and temperature.

She did a thorough job, then said, "Would you like to finish your picture now?"

Tilda nodded.

"I have a surprise for you. Come on, hop down." Sophie held out her arms to help, and when Tilda was once again sitting at the little desk, Sophie picked up an iPad with a set of headphones attached and said, "Do you like *Frozen*?"

"It's my *fay*bret!"

"Want to watch the best part while you color?" She set the tablet on the desk, the movie already queued, and then gently lowered a headset over Tilda's ears, and tapped the PLAY button.

Then she turned to Emily. "Those are noise cancelling headphones, so we can talk. First, just know that she's fine at the moment. There's no sign that the condition is active yet." Then she looked at Joe. "This is how it goes with this thing. There's nothing, there's nothing, there's nothing, and then all of the sudden there's something."

He nodded. "That's how it was with Dad. He was fine, and then he got sick, really sick, all at once."

Emily nodded. "Every time she gets so much as a hiccup, I start to panic," she said. "Her doctor in New Mexico said when the symptoms do begin, the disease progresses rapidly. Within days."

Sophie glanced down at Tilda, her expression gentle and kind. Tilda was completely absorbed in her movie. "Just remember, she's okay for now. We'll want to monitor her closely. And I'll get moving immediately on testing everyone in the family to find her a marrow donor." She shifted her gaze to Joey then. "Does the family know?"

"Just Jason and Rob. I'm calling a family meeting at high noon to break the news."

"You tell them to get their asses over here this afternoon to be tested. I'll move all my other appointments to tomorrow." She put a hand on Emily's shoulder. "Your little girl has just become my top priority. I'm going to do everything in my power. I know one of the top doctors in pediatric blood disorders, and he knows all the others. I'll call him as soon as we finish up here."

"Th-thank you." Emily barely knew what to say.

"She's family," Sophie said. "That's the way this family works. Call her doctor in New Mexico. You'll have to give permission for them to send me her files. Let them know I'll be contacting them later today."

"I will."

"How long are you staying in town?"

She shot a look at Joey, then at her little girl. "I...don't know."

"Oh." Sophie looked from one of them to the other.

"At least through the holidays," Joey said. And he looked at her as he said it. He didn't make it sound like a question, but in his eyes, it was.

"Yes, through the holidays and until we get the test results back. That's...I can't look any further ahead than that right now." Why did she feel like the ground beneath her feet was crumbling all over again? Had she been stupidly hoping this doctor would tell her something different?

She'd felt the same way when she'd first got the diagnosis. As if the very planet was just falling out from under her.

"What if..." she looked at Sophie, her eyes blurred with moisture. "What if no one's a match?"

"What if everyone is?" Sophie replied. She smiled gently. "Listen, I want you, both of you, to leave the medical stuff to me. Unload that from your shoulders, okay?"

Joey nodded. Emily nodded too, but it was a lie. There were a thousand options running through her mind. Clinical trials. New, European treatments not yet available in the states.

"You need to keep your heads in the here and now," Sophie went on. "She's not sick *right now*. Right now, she's just a normal three-and-a-half-year-old kid looking forward to Christmas. That's all. And that's where you need to be, too, until and unless there's a reason not to be. Do you think you can do that?"

Joey nodded hard. "I can. I will." He turned to look at Emily.

She gaped at him, then at Sophie. "I'm sorry, but... you just expect me to pretend my little girl doesn't have a terminal disease? Just pretend everything's normal?"

Joe frowned and said, "I know it's hard—"

"You don't know anything. You've known her for two days. She's my world, Joey. She's my *heart*."

Tilda looked their way suddenly, a beaming bright smile on

her face as she pulled the headset off, her attention span completely maxed out. Emily quickly turned around, so her little girl wouldn't see her tears, and at the same time, Joey scooped Tilda up and turned her a little bit away from her mom.

"Go ahead and fix your makeup, Emily," Dr. Sophie said. "Tilda and I need to finish this picture of hers."

Nodding, Em slipped out of the room and into the hallway. The tears flooded over out there, and she leaned back against the door, a hand cupped over her mouth to keep from sobbing out loud.

She couldn't live if she lost her little girl. She couldn't survive it.

Taking a deep, shuddering breath, she straightened up and made her way through the clinic in search of the restroom.

∽

Joey left Tilda and Sophie to finish coloring and went in search of Emily. He found her coming out of the restroom, eyes red but no tears in sight, gold and amber curls looking as if she'd run her hands through them a few times.

"Are you okay?"

She met his eyes, then looked at the floor. "I'm trying to be strong, I really am."

"You've shouldered this whole thing alone. You don't have to do that anymore. You need to break down now and then... I'll cover you. And I'm hoping you'll do the same for me."

She nodded, took a trembling breath, seemed to gather herself.

"I don't want to put more on you, Em, but...I want to be able to tell her I'm her daddy," he said. "I don't know what I did to make you think I don't deserve that little girl, but—"

She opened her mouth but he held up a hand. "I don't particularly care. I'll spend the rest of my life trying to prove you were wrong about me."

"Or the rest of hers," she whispered, and the damn tears tried to flood her pretty eyes all over again. She searched his face, though. "You really have changed."

"I've changed a little. Not as much in four years as I have in the last two days, though, I'll tell you that. And it's the truth. I was a kid back then. I'm a man now. I'm a *father* now." Holding her eyes, trying to show her his soul in his own, he said, "At least I want to be."

She didn't look away. It felt like she was stripping his soul bare, and scrutinizing his bones. "She already loves you," she said. "It'll be worse. Way worse if she knows and then you…" Her voice trailed off.

"Disappoint her?" he asked. "Hurt her like I apparently hurt you?"

She looked around the corner, into the room where Tilda sat, coloring with intense concentration. Her tongue was sticking out the corner of her mouth. "You can't, that's the thing. If we tell her, you can't hurt her. You understand? No matter what, no matter how hard it gets, whatever you start with her, you need to follow through. You can't change your mind."

"I swear to God, Emily, I'll put Matilda ahead of everything and everyone else in my life, always." He looked in at her, too, and felt all mushy over her round little cheeks and her lips, like a swollen valentine. "I'd jump in front of a train for her." His chest felt full again. It happened every time he looked at his little girl. It felt hard to breathe, and kind of close to bursting like an over-inflated balloon.

He dragged his eyes away to look at her mother, and suddenly glimpsed a mirror image of Matilda. Emily's high, perfect cheeks were not quite as round but the tip of her Tinkerbell nose was the same.

Some long-dormant tenderness for Emily stirred around in

his soul. *No. No... no*, he thought, giving the sleeping dragon a pat on its head. *You just go on back to sleep. Tilda's the focus now. Not her mamma.*

"Okay," she said softly.

Those two syllables snapped him back to attention. "Okay?"

"Yeah. I'll tell her you're her father."

He put both hands on her shoulders and held her eyes hard. He was the one doing the searching this time, trying to find evidence she really meant what she was saying. "Thank you. But *we'll* tell her. Together. All right?"

Her jaw tightened just a little. "I'm the only parent she's ever had, Joey. Right now, you're just a brand new friend in her life. I at least have to prepare her for the notion that she has a father."

"She's never asked?"

She averted her eyes. "She started to a couple of times. Just recently as a matter of fact. I just always sense it coming and steer her onto another topic."

He nodded. "Still, you're right. I didn't think about your way being easier on Tilda." Then he nodded. "You break the news first, if you want, and then...." He looked past her, searching space for an image that didn't come to him. "And then what?"

"And then we'll spend the day together, celebrating. Showing our little girl the time of her life, just like Doctor Sophie said." Then she added, "Just give me the rest of today with her, okay? I'll tell her this afternoon, and we'll meet in the morning."

"Okay." A smile pulled at his face. "It feels wrong to be so happy when she's so sick."

"Believe me, I know. There's this constant tug of war going on in my heart every minute of every day." Emily shrugged. "But Sophie was right. She's not sick yet. Maybe we should be as happy as we can for as long as we can."

"Yeah," he said, looking a bit longer at the prettiest little princess in the west.

Joey returned to the Long Branch, knowing he'd find his family there. His stepmother Vidalia was behind the bar wiping glasses, long dark curls with silver strands that looked like they'd been added on purpose, all pulled around to one side and held with a turquoise, Navajo style clip. As much as his father kept nudging at her to retire and travel with him, she loved her own saloon, the OK Corral, and her five daughters too much to go too far away. He'd have expected his father to have figured that out by now.

"You look like you've been rode hard and put away wet, boy," she said. She drew him a beer and slid it across the bar as he took a seat on a saddle shaped stool. "Girls," she called toward the back. "Joey's here!"

The two women who responded were her two youngest, Melusine, the PI, with her pixie short hair as dark as her mamma's and Selene, his half sister, with hair the color of the moon and Arctic blue eyes.

"Your brothers didn't want you to face a full-blown family meeting," Vidalia said. "I thought maybe the four of us could talk first."

Joey sighed, lowering his head. "I just...I don't want to have to tell this too many times."

"Landsakes, what's wrong?" Vidalia reached across the bar to clasp one of his hands between both of hers, and when he looked up, her eyes were wide with alarm.

Melusine moved up behind him and put a hand on his shoulder. Selene stood right where she was, just inside the swinging doors that led into the kitchen. She had that look on her face, the same one her mother and sister would be wearing in a minute. Like she already knew.

Hell, maybe she did.

"A few weeks ago," he said, "Matilda Louise was diagnosed with Sanguis Morbo."

"Oh, Lord, not again." Vidalia pressed a hand to her chest and closed her eyes.

"That's...that's what your father had," Mel whispered.

He nodded, turning to look at Selene. "She needs a bone marrow transplant to save her life. We all need to get tested. I mean the boys, and dad and I. And I was hoping you—"

"We'll *all* get tested," Selene said. She was the donor who'd saved his father's life, the daughter Bobby Joe had never known about until that Christmas two years ago.

God, Joey was dying to talk to his father about this. If anyone would understand his warring feelings of elation and anger, of joy and devastation, it would be him.

"Thanks, Selene." Then he looked at the women, at the tears in their eyes. "She isn't sick yet. Sophie says she might go a whole year before...any symptoms set in. Then again, it could happen any time. Once they do, it's...fast. So I need everyone to get on this. Sophie's cleared out her appointments today to make room for us."

"We'll do it today." Vidalia squeezed his hands. "I'll let everyone else know so you don't have to keep putting yourself through this."

"Thanks, Vidalia." He shook his head. "I wanted to tell Dad myself."

"That man's been acting off ever since Emily and Tilda arrived in town." She sighed. "No matter. You let me worry about your father."

Melusine sighed and slid onto the stool beside his. "Why did she keep Matilda from you for so long?"

"I don't know."

"You didn't *ask?*"

"We've had other priorities in the two days she's been in town, Mel."

"I guess, but—"

"It's okay," Selene said. "It's in the past. What we need to focus on now is getting her better."

"You're right," Vidalia said, reaching for her phone. "Joey, I'm going to activate my prayer circle."

Mel reached out a hand and said, *"Mom—"*

"No, no, that's good, Vidalia," Joey interrupted. "Let's throw everything we've got at this thing."

"Then I'll call the coven together," Selene said softly.

Vidalia rolled her eyes.

"You take care of your girl, Joey," Melusine said. "Let the family help out with everything else. We can take shifts at the Long Branch, we can babysit, and we can make sure you and Emily get fed and cared for while you deal with all this."

He said, "I think we both just want to give Tilda the best Christmas ever."

"Oh honey," Vidalia said, smiling gently. "Christmas is what we do *best*."

~

Tilda napped for her usual hour, and as always, woke up ravenous. By the time Emily convinced her to use the bathroom, wash her hands, and get dressed, she was pretty hungry herself.

"Well now," Ida Mae said as they came down the stairs, "that's not the same outfit you were wearing this morning, is it dear?"

"Nope." Tilda lifted her arms over her head, and turned in a complete circle, imitating a ballerina. She'd chosen a dress with a glittery purple tulle skirt, orange and yellow paisley print leggings, and her pink Converse high tops.

"I think that's the prettiest dress yet, Matilda Louise."

"Thank you," she said, smiling so hard her cheeks glowed.

"You hungry? I have your lunch all ready."

"Is it hot dogs?" Tilda asked in a hopeful tone.

"No."

"Oh." Tilda sighed, then added, "They ain't really made of dogs, you know."

Emily corrected, "They *aren't* really made from dogs."

"That's what I said."

Ida Mae served them in the sunroom again, though it was shady out there in the afternoon. Tuna salad sandwiches on toasted bread triangles with the crusts removed and homemade chicken noodle soup.

It was so good Emily wondered if she would ever want to cook for herself again. Ida Mae was an artist. She told her so before the happy innkeeper headed back inside and gave them their space.

Emily watched her daughter eat, and even managed to eat her own meal. She wasn't sick with worry about telling Tilda that Joey was her father. It felt like the right thing. She wasn't worried that Joey would try to take Tilda away. Not anymore. She believed him when he said he wanted to put the past behind them and focus on Tilda, and on giving her a wonderful Christmas and on finding a cure that would ensure many more. It felt right to tell her little girl the truth.

What felt wrong was the time she had let pass before doing so. But it hadn't felt wrong, not until the past two days. Now that she was in Big Falls, though, she was starting to think she had made a terrible mistake all those years ago.

"I have a surprise for you, Tilda."

She widened her eyes, clapped her hands, and quickly looked all around the table, then under it. "I don't see it!"

"Well, it's not that kind of surprise. It's…something I have to tell you."

Tilda pouted. "That's not a very good s'prise."

"Don't be so sure."

Sighing heavily, crossing her arms and tipping her head, she said, "Okay. Tell me." Her voice dripped as much doubt as a three-year-old's voice could carry.

"You have a daddy."

Tilda's little eyebrows rose as high as they could go. "I *do*?"

"Mm-hm."

"Is he here?" She looked through the open doors into the main part of the house.

"No, but you've met him. It's Joey."

"*Joey*? Is my *daddy*?" She clapped her little hands over her mouth, like she was trying to hold in the squeal that erupted anyway. Then she was off the chair and running around the sunroom, singing "Joey's my dad, Joey's my dad, I have a dad and Joey's my dad!"

The double doors swung open and Ida Mae stood there with a plate of apple pie in each hand. She sort of smiled, or maybe it was a grimace, met Emily's eyes, and said, "I'm so sorry. I didn't mean—"

"It's all right, Ida Mae. Joey's family knows and I'm sure it'll be all over town within a few days anyway."

"Actually, dear, it already is." She set the pie on the table.

"Why din't he *tell* me?" Tilda asked.

"He wanted to. I asked him to let me tell you myself."

"Why?"

She shrugged. "I don't know. I thought it would be better for you."

"Can he come over?"

It hadn't fazed her. She wasn't upset. Eventually, when she got old enough to think of such things, she would have questions. Where had Joey been all this time? Why hadn't he been with her? Why hadn't Emily told her sooner?

Emily wasn't going to come out looking very good when she answered those questions. Her little girl might not like her very much for a while, once she learned the truth. God, she'd dug herself into a pit there was no getting out of, hadn't she?

And yet Joey wasn't without blame.

Unless he was.

"Can he, Mommy?"

"We're going to spend the whole day together tomorrow."

"Do we have to wait that long?"

Em sighed, recognizing the longing in her baby's eyes. It wasn't in her to refuse Tilda anything. "I'll find out," she said, and picked up her phone. She dialed his number.

He picked up before the first ring finished. "Emily?"

She tapped a button. "You're on speaker. I just told Tilda the news, and she wants to talk to you."

She held out the phone, nodded at her daughter.

"Hi, Daddy," Tilda said, smiling ear to ear.

"Hello—" his voice caught, broke, he cleared his throat. "Hello, Tilda."

She giggled. "Can you come over?"

"I could. Can I talk to your mom for a minute?"

"Okay." She pushed the phone away, and Emily tapped the icon again and brought it to her ear.

"Go ahead, you're not on speaker."

"She sounds okay with it so far," he said.

"She's kind of delighted with it so far. And she doesn't want to wait for tomorrow to see you." She took a deep breath. "I was wrong, Joey," she said very softly. "I should have let you be here. We should have told her together." She wondered then how many other times she'd been wrong in the decisions she'd made about Tilda and her father.

"You don't know how good that makes me feel," he said. "That she's happy and wants to see me, not that you admitted you were wrong."

"A little bit that I admitted I was wrong," she said.

"Maybe a little bit. Listen, we have a thing going on here tonight that she might enjoy."

"At the Long Branch?"

"Yeah. We're decorating the tree. New tradition, inspired by the way the town decorates the one in the park. Everyone brings an ornament to hang. At seven we turn on the lights and sing carols for an hour. Done by eight. We don't serve alcohol until after that. It's a family thing. Do you want to bring her?"

She found herself nodding. "Yeah, I do. It sounds beautiful, Joey."

"It is. I'm glad you're coming."

"Me too. Here, you can tell her yourself." She put the phone back on speaker. "Go ahead."

"Hey, Tilda?"

"What?"

"I'll see you real soon, okay? Put on your most Christmassy dress. You and your mom are coming over for a Christmas Tree decorating party."

"Yay!" She dove out of the chair. It rocked, and Emily dropped the phone to grab it before it could fall. Tilda was halfway up the stairs yelling, "I need a Christmassy dress!" while Joey was yelling, "What happened? You girls okay?" from the phone.

Shaking her head, Emily recovered the phone, and said, "Fine, fine. She shot off like a rocket to find a dress. I've gotta go."

"That made her happy, then?"

"It made her very happy. Thank you, Joey."

"Anytime. If you want to come early, dinner's on me."

"Tell me you have hot dogs."

"I guarantee you, I will have."

CHAPTER SIX

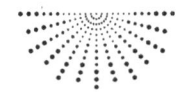

The community room at Vidalia's church was decked in white lights and garland, with an artificial tree near one wall and a five-foot-long framed replica of *The Last Supper* on another. Already, gifts, donated by locals, were piled under the tree and more dangled from its needled boughs. On Christmas Eve, they'd be delivered to the less fortunate residents of Big Falls and outlying communities.

Tonight, the room was also filled with a couple dozen women and a handful of men. Vidalia wondered, and not for the first time, why women always seemed to be so far ahead of the curve, spiritually speaking.

There were cafeteria-style tables and folding chairs. One table, by the wall, held the church's coffee urn (she'd brought her own coffee) and slices of her homemade peach upside down cake with hand-whipped cream on top. She could give Sunny a run for her money, she thought.

Vidalia moved to the front of the room with a mug of coffee in her hand and a smile on her face, despite the deep ache in her heart.

"I just love you all so much for coming out tonight," she said, looking around the room. Her daughters weren't there. They were busy young women, all of them. The prayer group was made up of the more mature segment of Big Falls. The elder-women, and a couple of men, who formed the core members of the congregation. Those old enough to have learned the miraculous power of prayer and who knew how to wield it.

A wave of mutters, a few words rising above the rest, then they settled again. Forks scraped china—Vidalia Brand McIntyre did not serve on paper plates—but aside from that, the room was silent.

"You've probably heard I have a new grandchild, Matilda Louise. New to me, at least."

"Pretty little thing," Rosie called. She ran the diner. "Those eyes of hers could melt a glacier."

"Smart as a whip, too," Ida Mae put in.

Vidalia nodded. "Thank you. She's a blessing, a gift to us." She lowered her eyes, tried to find words. She didn't want pity. She wanted action. "She's sick, friends." Everyone gasped or exclaimed as she gave her words time to sink in. "It's the same ailment that nearly took her grandpa, my darlin' Bobby Joe, two Christmases ago. She needs a bone marrow transplant. And so far, her doctors are having a hard time finding a match. So…I think it's time we call on a higher authority to step in."

"Amen!" Betty Lou Jennings shouted. She had a voice that always surprised folks, it was so high pitched and childlike. "And after that, we'll do a donor drive. We'll get everyone in town tested!"

"Great idea!"

"I'll get tested!"

"I'll put the word out at Sunday's service," Pastor Jackson said.

Vidalia nodded, her heart filling. She loved her church, its members, and her town. "You can get tested over at the clinic. If we get more than my sweet niece Sophie can handle, she'll make arrangements with Tucker Lake General to take the overflow."

Everyone nodded, and Vidalia caught the pastor's eye. "Would you lead us in prayer for Matilda Louise, Pastor Jackson?"

He got to his feet, plate in hand, and said, "Only if I can have another piece of this cake afterwards."

Everyone laughed softly, and the pastor took to the front of the room. They bowed their heads, and he led them in prayer. His words were simple and heartfelt and powerful because of that.

Vidalia felt her eyes start to burn as he spoke to the Lord on little Tilda's behalf, and her breath hitched in her lungs a bit. But she felt more than that. She felt the power of God filling that room and bathing everyone in its light. It started out as just a subtle sensation, but then that sensation got bigger. She felt it grow, as if faith was beaming from everyone whose head was bent in prayer. In her mind's eye, Vidalia imagined those smaller beams blending into a greater glow, and with every addition, the light of God's love became bigger and brighter and stronger. If she opened her eyes, she knew she would see it. But she wasn't going to open her eyes, because this was about faith. This was about believing what couldn't be seen.

Pastor Jackson said amen, and everyone repeated the word. "Amen," Vidalia whispered, and she opened her eyes.

For the briefest of instants, a millionth of a millionth of a second, that stunning glow she'd sensed was visible. And then the room looked normal again, only somehow...lighter. And every face in it seemed lighter as well.

She took in a deep breath, then let it all out, every bit of it. It was going to be okay. Somehow it was going to be okay.

~

Tilda wore her Christmas dress. It had a red velvet skirt and white lace sleeves, and glitter made its white bodice sparkle like snow. With her softly falling curls and huge brown eyes, she looked just like a Christmas angel.

She smoothed her skirt nervously as they stood just outside the entrance to the Long Branch Saloon. It had a big, garland-trimmed exterior door with a giant wreath covering its glass entirely. They walked through it and into an entry hall with benches along the walls and pegs for hanging up coats. At the far end of that area, a set of batwing doors led into the dim interior of the barroom. Emily could see strings of multicolored lights and lots of human silhouettes. There were myriad muttering voices.

Then a piano started to play a familiar riff, and voices rose in a happily off-pitch version of "Deck the Halls."

Matilda looked up at her mom with a smile. Emily smiled back, and took off Tilda's coat to hang it up beside her own. "Ready?" She held out her hand.

Her little girl clutched it, nodded, and they walked on through. People parted to let them pass, and it felt to Emily like every last one of them knew who she was, who Matilda was.

Joey shouldered his way through the throng to meet them, scooped Matilda right up in one arm, and put the other one around Emily's shoulders. "Glad you made it," he said. "Sorry it's so crowded. It's a big night around here." He talked as he steered her back the way he'd come, until they crossed the wide threshold into the dining room half of the place.

"They started the caroling early?" Emily asked.

"Spontaneous eruptions of holiday spirit cannot be scheduled," he replied.

The whole time, she was trying to figure out if she should object to his arm around her shoulders. But before she could decide, he'd lowered it to his side again and was looking at Tilda's face. "There's our tree, Tilda. What do you think?"

Emily glanced at the pine tree on the far side of the room, taking up two stories of the place. It had to be twenty feet tall. She'd seen it her first time here, but she'd been too distracted by other things to pay it much attention. She looked back at Tilda and saw her wide-eyed wonder.

"Woooooow," she said.

"We're gonna decorate it and then turn on the lights."

Tangles and webs of lights were tucked into, over, under and around every bough. But not yet glowing.

"I brought a declaration," Tilda said.

"Decoration, hon," Em corrected.

"That's what I said." Tilda looked over at Emily, and so did Joey.

Emily got stuck like a skipping record for a second, her gaze jumping back and forth between Joey's eyes and Tilda's. Something whispered through her. A memory, maybe. And fear, as it hit her yet again, maybe even more deeply than before, that Matilda Louise was as much his as hers, physically, genetically, not just legally.

"Did you forget it, Mommy?"

"Oh! Um, no, of course not." Joey was still gazing at her, though, his head tipped to one side, kind of a speculative look in his eyes and one gorgeous eyebrow cocked up just slightly higher than the other. Inquisitive and cute as hell. That look had always got to her.

She snapped out of it and yanked her bag off her shoulder, bending over it to dig around inside. And she found what she was looking for. A carefully wrapped bundle, which she pulled out and unwrapped.

Two pine cones dangled from loops of red yarn, each one decorated to within an inch of its life. They sparkled under layers of red and green glitter. Individual dried cranberries had been hot glued here and there, along with plastic holly leaves trimmed in frosty white.

"Hoo-boy. Did you make those?" Joey asked, staring at the pine cones Emily was holding up and inadvertently past them and into her eyes. She wanted to look away and couldn't.

"I made that one." Tilda poked one of the pinecones, and it swung right into Emily's nose, breaking the hold Joey's eyes had on hers.

"Hey!" Em said, rubbing her nose and giving her kid a fake scowl.

Tilda giggled "Sorry, Mommy," but the words got lost in her laughter.

Someone tapped Joey on the shoulder, and Em saw Vidalia behind him.

"This way," she said. "We saved you a seat." She smiled a hello to Em, then beamed one at Matilda before turning to lead the way back to the huge section of pushed-together tables. Em recognized Maya and Kara, and their children. She knew Kiley and Rob and Doc Sophie and her son Max. There were others— the rest of Vidalia's daughters. She wondered which was Selene, the half sister.

Then she looked straight into the eyes of Bobby Joe McIntyre, and she stopped. Everything in her went cold.

She had known Joey's father would be there. She had been dreading the moment she would have to see that man again. And now it had arrived, and she was nowhere near ready.

But he was up on his feet, and then the other men at the table were too. "Everyone," Joey said, "this is Emily Hawkins."

Everyone said hello and his father added, "You look wonderful, Emily. It's so good to see you again."

The liar.

"And this," Joey said, bouncing Tilda a little, "is Matilda Louise. My daughter."

"Me first, me first." Vidalia was closest, but not too close. She stood in front of him and Tilda and nodded at him. "Go on, tell her who I am." She was so excited she was bouncing in place. Vidalia, not Tilda.

"I already know you," Tilda said. "You're Dahlia's gramma."

"And your gramma, too, Tilda."

"What?" She looked at Vidalia and rounded her eyes dramatically, like she must have seen someone do on TV. She just picked up everything. "I have a gramma!?"

"And a grandpa," Vidalia said, waving across the table to the far end where Bobby Joe was still standing. He didn't come around the table, and Vidalia frowned at him a little.

Emily knew why, though. He'd seen the look in her eyes a second ago, telling him if he laid a finger on her daughter, she would rip it off.

She didn't know if anyone else had noticed it, and she didn't particularly care. Pasting a smile back onto her face, she moved to one of the empty seats that flanked a tall wooden booster chair, and slid onto it. Joey started to put Tilda into her seat, and she twisted, and said, "I'm a big girl! I don't need a high chair!"

He stopped moving and said, "Okay, sure. I'll sit there if you want." Then he put her in his own seat.

She looked extremely pleased with herself. Emily could almost see her brilliant little brain computing this newfound knowledge. *This one is completely in my control.* She could take over the world with information like that.

She opened her mouth to say something, but Joey was pulling out the high chair so he could step around it. It didn't have a tray like a baby's high chair. It was just a slightly taller, skinnier seat than the others. He backed his rear end up to it. Of course, he wouldn't fit. The chair's arms were too close together. But he kept moving all the same, trying again and again to shove his butt into the too-small opening, and Tilda was laughing so hard little squeals were squeaking out in between. Her face was turning red and her giggles were infectious.

Maya's twins joined in. And then Kara's Tyler started cracking up, and one by one every adult in the place was laughing.

She was even laughing.

"Daddy, you won't fit!" Tilda giggle-shouted.

Everyone stopped laughing at once, and Emily looked around. Several hands were either pressed to hearts or dabbing at eyes. Vidalia leaned her head onto her evil husband's shoulder, her eyes pooling. But then Emily realized Joey's eyes were on her, and she turned and met them and saw how wet they were. She'd called him daddy just like it was the most natural thing in the world. His eyes pleaded with her to say something, and she got the message that he couldn't trust himself to speak just then.

"Well, Tilda," Emily said. "I don't see any other chairs. And I think you're the only one who will fit in that chair."

Nodding hard, Tilda slid down out of Joey's seat, clasped his hand, and pushed him toward the chair. She climbed up into the high chair all by herself, though Emily's hands shot instinctively toward her several times. She made it. On her own.

Once Tilda was settled in, Emily relaxed, leaned back in her chair. She saw Maya, mother of the twins Dahlia and Cal, smiling her way and asked, "When does the independent phase end?"

Maya shrugged and looked at Kara. Kara glanced at Tyler and smiled. "I'll let you know."

"No, *I'll* let you *all* know," Sophie said, elbowing teenage Max who sat beside her.

Introductions were made all around. She met the three of Vidalia's daughters she hadn't met before, Melusine, Edain and Selene. A waitress brought a dinner plate with hot dogs and french fries for Tilda, and others brought platters of cookies and pitchers of hot cocoa around, leaving several of each at every table. People filled mugs and took cookies. Others had congregated around the piano, and were singing carols in imperfect harmony.

One by one, people wandered up to the tree to hang whatever ornament they'd brought. There was a ladder on either side, staff standing on top to place ornaments safely on the highest boughs. People ate and talked and laughed. And they didn't stay in one place either; they were milling around, wandering to each other's tables, visiting.

It hit her what a really unique place Big Falls was. A friendly small town where everyone knew everyone else. It was truly something special.

"We should socialize, Mom," Maya said to Vidalia. "We look all cliquish over here."

"Yeah, we're the hosts," said Edain. She was beautiful, like movie star beautiful. She wore a one-shoulder black dress and sat beside a man who rocked a pair of faded jeans and a blue plaid western shirt with pearl buttons.

The blonde caught her staring and smiled. "I'm dying to get to know you better, Emily. We'll have time to visit after we've taken the first shift mingling." She took her husband's arm, and they both rose.

"Nice to meet you, Emily. You too, Matilda," her husband Wade said.

Tilda loved the formality of all that, and said, "Nice to meet you, too," over pronouncing the T's.

"Save us some cookies," Edie said, and the two of them wove through the patrons, pausing to chat up each person they came to.

"We'll join them," Kara said. "Tyler?"

"I'll stay here," Tyler replied with a quick look from his mom to his dad, who wore a police uniform. Jim something.

"Okay," Kara told him. "Help out with the other kids."

Emily thought Kara was brilliant. Tyler grew three inches taller at those words. The two of them left the table to circulate among the guests. It was odd to see a family she'd grown up knowing, with this entirely new branch. The Brands and the McIntyres acted like a family that had been united for decades.

Personally, she thought she was going to need flash cards to keep them all straight.

She sat uneasily, trying to listen, but all their words blended into a friendly drone. She just nodded and smiled, not really hearing any of it. She felt every set of eyes though. They took turns gazing adoringly and sadly at her daughter and then curiously at her. Those stares felt probing, questioning, but none were judging or disapproving. They knew what she'd done to Joey. They had no idea why.

One of them knew why, she thought, glancing at Bobby Joe. He was looking very guilty. He ought to, the bastard.

And then her mind gently corrected her. Two people at this table knew why she'd done what she had. Two. Joey knew.

She'd believed all this time that he'd known, anyway.

If she was wrong about that...then she was possibly the worst human being on planet Earth.

∼

Something was going on between Emily and his father. Joey wondered if it was as obvious to everyone else at the table as it was to him. He'd never seen his father so quiet at a family gathering. Bobby Joe slumped in his chair like an old man. Even Vidalia was sending him questioning glances every little while. He kept looking at Joey, and then at Matilda Louise, and his eyes were red and had lines of tension and strain at the corners. He seemed to avoid looking at Emily at all, which was weird.

Joey glanced at Emily and noticed her doing the same thing, looking everywhere except at his father, and when her gaze did stray Bobby Joe's way once or twice, it turned as dark as an Oklahoma storm cloud.

Other than that odd note, the evening went really well. Emily and Tilda Lou hung their ornaments on the tree. The player piano struck up a carol every ten minutes or so, and everyone sang along. Neighbors stopped by the table to meet the newest Big Falls residents, to welcome them. Sunny from the bakery came over. She glanced Jason's way, and beamed a little brighter when he glanced back. Their soft smiles told him something was definitely brewing between the two of them.

In fact, things were almost perfect until Dax Russell sort of crashed through the batwing doors into the all but empty bar. All the patrons were on the dining room side. He stood still for a minute, looking around, blinking as he seemed to orient himself.

"Jeeze, Dax looks like a lost Viking or something," Kiley said, getting up and heading his way with Rob right on her heels.

Dax waved a hand at her and stumbled onto a stool at the unmanned bar. He thumped the hardwood with a fist. "Wuzzah guy gotta do to gitta beer aroun' here?"

Rob glanced behind him at the family and mouthed, "Sorry."

Joey excused himself and went over to help his brother out. This was his place now in every way that counted. Besides, everything in him bristled at the notion of Dax, sweet as he was sober, being anywhere near Tilda Louise in this condition. He'd tried to keep his promise to Kiley, but Dax hadn't returned his calls. He'd been planning to drive out to see him, but, well, things happened.

Kiley was talking to Dax, telling him she'd take him somewhere he could lie down, and Dax was mouthing off loudly. Rob was there and about to step in. Joe clasped his shoulder, and he looked back. "I got this," Joe said.

Rob nodded. "He's a friend. Go easy."

Joey nodded, then stepped up in front of Dax. "You're drunk. My family's here. My *kid* is here. This is not okay."

"I'll go get a room key," Kiley said, hurrying toward the back.

"Number three's empty," Rob called after her as she dashed through the doors and into the kitchen that led to the attached office.

Dax blinked. "I'm not that drunk."

"My place, my call," Joey said. "You can either sleep it off upstairs or in one of Jim's cells in town. You pick." He glanced back at the table and saw that Jimmy's eyes were on the situation, as focused as a cougar on a bunny.

Joe gave him a nod to tell him he could relax, but he knew Jim wouldn't, not until the situation was eased. He started to get up, and Dax apparently wasn't too drunk to notice, and quickly got off the stool. "Okay, okay, I'll take a room upstairs."

"Good."

Kiley returned with the key. "We'll take him up," she said.

"Yeah, go ahead back to your family." Rob pulled Dax's arm around his shoulders.

"Thanks," Joey said.

The two of them supported Dax between them up the stairs. The crowd in the dining room resumed talking and laughing. Three steps up, Dax lifted his head and bellowed, "Joey has a *kid*?"

Joey winced and shot a look Emily's way. But she wasn't in her seat, and he glanced around the table as everyone resumed talking and laughing. Vidalia was in Joey's vacated spot having an animated conversation with Tilda and *beaming* with joy. Bobby Joe wasn't in his spot, either.

Narrowing his eyes, Joey scanned the place, and then he saw them, in the little hallway that led back to the restrooms, not twenty feet from where he was.

He moved quickly their way, because it was clear they were arguing.

"...no matter what happens, you will never put your hands on my little girl. Never!" Emily said.

She sensed him there as she finished her threat, and her eyes shifted toward him.

Bobby Joe didn't see him yet, and his reply was fervent. "Emily, whatever you may think of me, you need to believe what I told you. Joey never knew."

Joe stepped closer, revealing himself to his father. "What are you talking about, Dad? What didn't I know?"

His father stared at him for a long moment, then said, "We'll talk later. I hope. But I'm gonna leave now. Tell Vidalia I was overtired, just needed to go home."

"Don't leave on our account," Emily snapped. Then she turned to Joey, her eyes sparking. "I need to take Tilda and go."

He nodded. He still didn't know what the hell was going on, but his father headed for the exit, and he knew it was something major. "She's been waiting for the tree-lighting," he said. "I told her she could throw the switch." His voice was hoarse with worry. What the hell was going on?

They both looked toward the table. Vidalia was teaching Tilda "Oh Little Playmate" and practically glowing. Emily swallowed hard, he heard it. "You really don't know what's going on, do you?"

"Between you and my father? No clue, Em, but I don't like it."

She nodded slowly, but then looked past him at Tilda Lou. "Then I need to tell you. But not here."

He nodded. "Let's wrap things up, then." He didn't like the feelings inside him. Clearly his father had kept something from him, and he couldn't think of very many things it might have been. It was something to do with Emily. And there was only one theory that came to mind.

He could not imagine his father knowing that Joey had a child and keeping it secret. He couldn't imagine it.

He walked Emily back to the table, his hand on her elbow. She eased into her chair, trying to force a normal expression, but his cousins saw right through it. The men were oblivious, but those Brand girls could read a face a half mile away.

"Everything all right, Joey?" Vidalia asked, her dark eyes hopping from him to Em and back again. "Where's your father?"

"Too many cookies, I think," Joey said. "He said he'd see you at home." Then he clapped his hands together, "You ready to light up that Christmas tree, Miss Matilda Louise?"

"Yes!" She put down the cookie she'd been eating, stood up in her chair and reached for him.

"Wait, wait," Emily shot to her feet, quick-drawing wet wipes from her bag like a seasoned gunfighter.

He'd already grabbed Tilda, though, panicking that she'd fall out of the chair if he didn't, and she was squeezing his cheeks between her chocolate coated hands and saying, "This is the best Christmas ever!"

Emily peeled one of Tilda's hand off his face to wipe it clean with an expert swipe, then repeated the trick with the other one, and then she gave a quick swipe around her little mouth. It was all one motion, long practiced and perfect. It would've taken him ten minutes to get all the goo off.

Then she plucked a few more wipes and leaned in to wipe the chocolate off his cheeks, still smiling.

She was so beautiful when she smiled like that. He recognized the effect Tilda had on her mother. It was the same effect she had on him. Everything else just dissolved when she had his attention. Resentment, anger, impatience, worry, fear. All of it just melted away.

Emily had been furious a second ago; now she was smiling as serenely as an angel and gently dabbing chocolate handprints from his cheeks.

Her eyes moved just enough to meet his, and he looked into them for as long as she let him.

Then she blinked and stepped away.

He adjusted Tilda at his waist, and carried her over to the main switches on the wall.

"Turn the round button that way," he said, pointing with his thumb. "That way is left. Did you know that?"

"I know left and right, but not which is which."

"Hold up your hands," he told her. She did, and he spread her fingers out, and then traced her left forefinger down the outside and out along her inner thumb. "That's an L. L is for left."

She frowned and held up her other hand. "That's an L, too."

"No, that's a backwards L."

"It's a upside-down seven," she added, turning her hand downward.

"Okay, so left is never the upside down seven. Got it?"

She nodded hard and reached for the dimmer switch, then turned it slowly. As the lights went down, she said "ooooh" and cranked it the other way, making them, brighter, then dimmer, then brighter, then all the way dark, then blinding.

"Okay, okay, okay. You're gonna give people convulsions."

"What's that?"

He couldn't stand how cute she was. It was adorable. "I'll explain that another time. Now, just slowly turn the lights down until I say stop, and then leave them there so you can turn on the tree. Okay?"

"Okay." She put her hand on the dial and watched him, utterly focused.

"Go ahead, nice and slow."

She turned the dial slowly and the lights went down lower and lower. "Okay, stop," he said just before it was too dark to see.

He moved her a couple of inches, touched the wall switch and said, "All you have to do is flip this switch. You know how to do that?"

"Mm-hm," she said, nodding and putting her fingers on the switch.

"Okay. But before you do it, look at the tree."

She turned her head and flipped the switch. The tree lit up, and she squealed and hugged his neck.

Joey's chest filled up, and he had to close his eyes to keep the tears from spilling over. Someone started singing "O Christmas Tree," and he carried her closer to the twinkling pine. She snuggled into his arms and sang along as best she could. He wished someone was recording her sweet little voice, singing the words "O Christmas tree" over and over. She laid her head on his shoulder and he looked back at Emily, who was staring at him and tearing up a little herself. And little Tilda grew heavier in his arms, her body entirely relaxed.

He inclined his head, and Em got up and came to him. "She's asleep, isn't she?"

Em nodded. "Out like a light."

"I'll drive you home. I can walk back. It's a nice night for it."

"Okay."

CHAPTER SEVEN

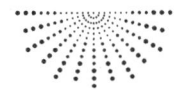

Joey leaned into the car, unfastened the buckles and scooped Tilda out. Emily closed the car door behind him. She had a key for the front door of the boarding house and opened it ahead of him.

Miss Ida Mae was in the foyer when they walked in, her tender gaze on Joey and the toddler in his arms, her expression all sweet and soft. She didn't say a word but gave them a little finger wave as they passed by, blowing a kiss to Tilda Lou.

He carried Tilda up the broad, perfect staircase. The curving hardwood railing gleamed and the carpet under his boots made him feel guilty for not pulling them off on the porch. The whole place smelled clean and citrusy. They reached the tall wooden door, and Emily used her antique key again. She hurried inside, turning on the smallest lamp in the room, a *Gone-with-the-Wind* style hurricane lamp.

She pulled back the covers of the most inviting bed he thought he'd ever laid eyes on. Everything about it was white and fluffy. It was like a cloud.

He lowered his girl into the bed, then crouched on the floor to carefully untie and wiggle off her little shoes. Tiny, pink

Converse high tops. Smiling, he whispered, "Nice, touch, Mom." And then he peeled off Tilda's socks, and frowned at the little patterns they left in her chubby calves. "Is that—"

"Normal. Perfectly normal."

He pulled the blanket over her, then straightened and looked at Emily. "Thank you for bringing her back to me."

She looked at him for a long time, standing there beside the bed. "I didn't have a choice, or I might not have. And I think that would've been a mistake...if you really didn't know about her this whole time."

"I didn't know," he said. "But my father did, didn't he?"

Holding his gaze, she nodded. And when his eyes and hers started touching in a way that was a little too familiar, she turned quickly away, opened a dresser drawer and pawed around inside.

"He offered me fifty grand to have an abortion." She said it like she was sharing the weather forecast. Like it didn't drive a black blade of betrayal right into his spine.

"He *said* that to you? That he'd pay you to—"

"Not to me, to my father." She pulled out a sweet pink nightgown and moved past him to the bed, peeling back those fluffy covers. "I told my father I was pregnant. He promised he'd take care of everything. I was such a coward that I couldn't face you myself. I was so afraid you and your family would think..."

"You thought we'd think it was deliberate. Because we're so wealthy."

She nodded. "Daddy assured me I was right. But he said he'd talk to your father. Later that same day, he handed it to me. Stacks of cash all strapped together in colored bands. I could smell the ink, you know? Like it was new."

"What exactly did your father say to you about the money?"

She peeled Tilda's dress over her head without jiggling her much at all, and in seconds, the nightgown had replaced it, and she was straightening it around her chubby legs, and then tucking the covers around her again. When she finished, she just sat there looking down at Tilda's sleeping face, stroking her hair. "You don't believe me, do you?"

"I just want all the information before I confront my father."

She turned and met his eyes, nodding slowly. She got up onto her feet, and picked up what looked like a small walkie talkie from a charger base. "Let's go outside, all right?" She nodded toward the suite's sitting room, and he saw the french doors in the back. "Do you want a drink?"

"Do you *have* a drink?"

"Yeah." She walked into the next room, unlocked a cabinet, and took out two glasses and a bottle of burgundy wine. "It was waiting in the room, when we arrived. That Ida Mae knows how to treat her guests, right?"

"Sure does." He came and took the bottle from her, expertly removed its cork, and filled the glasses, giving the bottle a little twist at the end to prevent dripping. He handed one to her, then followed her through the doors and outside. The balcony was big enough to hold a small iron table with two matching chairs, all painted white, and a fern that probably ought to go inside soon.

He didn't sit though. He leaned on the railing, looking out over the back yard. There were gardens out beyond the swing set, through a little white gated archway. Paths wound all through them, though most of the plants were dead or dying. It was December after all. Over the hills, Christmas lights gleamed bright from almost every house in sight.

Emily set the walkie talkie on the table and stood at the railing beside him, took a bracing sip of wine, then said, "My father handed me the money and said he knew it would be hard for me to end my pregnancy, but that everyone agreed it would be for the best. He said that the money was to make up for what I was going through and would help me with my education."

Joey felt her pain, knew it had been a horrible moment for

her. Maybe the most horrible moment she'd had, up to then. God knew she'd had worse since. That day in her doctor's office, getting the news that was a mother's nightmare. She shouldn't have had to face it alone. He should've been there, in both cases. But he hadn't known.

"We argued," she said. "I asked if he was seriously asking me to get rid of his grandchild. He said he couldn't stand to see me throw my life away. Like living my life for that little angel in there could ever be considered a waste." She thinned her lips, shook her head. "I cursed him. I yelled at him. I told him to keep your father's money, let it comfort him in his old age, because he no longer had a daughter to do it. And he certainly wouldn't have grandchildren. Not ever." She closed her eyes, took a healthy gulp from her glass. "And then I stormed out."

Joey turned to face her. "I'm so sorry, Em."

She was still staring out at the stars, the night. "I went back later that night. I was going to pack up my things and leave." She lowered her head. "And that's when I found him."

"That's when you...oh my God, Emily. That was the night your father died?"

She nodded. "My last words to him were shouted in anger. I'll never have the chance to make that right."

He put his arms around her, and she came to him. It felt natural, normal. He held her, and she cried. Warm tears soaked through his shirt, touching his skin. He stroked her hair and ached for her pain.

"I couldn't see you or your family again. I just couldn't. I was sure you knew. Daddy made it sound like you'd been a part of the whole conversation.

"I wasn't."

"As soon as he was buried, I went back to New Mexico. I left the money in the donation box at the Shrine of Our Lady of Guadalupe in Santa Fe, with a note. 'You owe me one, Mother

Mary.' Funny, right? Like someone out there really had the power to do anything for me."

"You used to believe in...things like that."

"I don't believe in anything, not anymore." She sniffled, and lifted her head from his shirt to look up at him. Her puffy, wet eyes broke his heart. "I couldn't give the money back to your family. I never wanted you or your father to know I hadn't done what... what I'd been paid to do."

"Thank God you didn't," he said. He put a palm against her cheek. "Thank God you carried her, you gave her life. You took care of her. On your own, you did all that."

She closed her eyes. "I owe you for the years you missed."

"I owe you for the years I wasn't there to help you, to take care of you and our little girl." Her tears were spilling over and his eyes were welling up too. "If I hadn't been the guy I was, you would never have believed I knew about her and didn't care."

"You were a kid."

"So were you." He stared into her eyes. "But I'm here now, Em. I'm here now. And I'm not going anywhere."

Then he lowered his mouth to hers, and he tasted the salt of tears on her lips when he kissed her.

∽

He tasted the same. He cupped the back of her head, kind of cradling it, just the way he used to. Every memory came crashing back to her, every delicious sensory detail about the way it used to be with them. Minutia she thought she'd forgotten, but they'd only been dormant, frozen in cryogenic stasis.

They were real again now. He had the softest lips, yielding, moving so gently. Like they were imbibing her. Like she was air to him.

He kissed her like Romeo kissed Juliet the night they said

goodbye. He kissed her like that every single time. Like he couldn't help himself.

She went soft against him, sinking into his arms. They were muscled steel, the armor worn by his soul. It felt good to surrender herself to the embrace of someone stronger. It felt good to lean. To be held. And it felt even better to try on this new belief. To try and think he really hadn't known.

He looked down into her eyes, searching for something. For the old Emily, maybe. She didn't think he'd find her. Hell, she didn't think *she* could find her.

"I wish things had been different," he said. "Maybe we'd have been together all this time."

She lowered her head quickly, a sheer knee-jerk reaction. "No. We wouldn't've been. I had to be in New Mexico taking classes, or I wouldn't have the Vetmobile right now."

"I'd have gone with you."

"You'd have come here anyway, to be with your dad when you almost lost him. If you hadn't, you wouldn't have the Long Branch. You'd have missed out on knowing the whole giant, overwhelming, too-decent-to-hate, Big Falls branch of your family." She blinked, gave her head a shake. "They're a hell of a bunch of women. You know that, right?"

"Of course I do." He shrugged. "Goodness sort of shines from a woman. It's what pulled me out to that pool I hated, summer night after summer night when you and your girlfriends would sneak in to go swimming." He clasped her shoulders, stepped back a little to look at her from arm's length. "You glow, Emily Hawkins. You always have, and I imagine you always will."

Then he grinned. "Tilda has it, too."

"You think Tilda made the moon, don't you?"

He glanced back into the suite, through the still-open bedroom door, at the sleeping angel in the big bed. "And the sun and the stars and all the planets. Don't you?"

"I do. I feel like I was born the day she was."

He nodded, and she knew he felt the same. She felt the empathic connection between them. There was a bond, now, wasn't there? A bond between them as Tilda's mother and her father. Not a romantic one, and not even a bond like friendship is a bond, but a bond of being goofy in love with their little girl.

"I'm sorry," she said. "I'm so sorry. I should've come to you, I should've faced you, but I was just…"

"Heartbroken," he said. "Alone, and young and pregnant, and thinking I knew and didn't care. You would've come around in a few days, once you'd had time to think. But then you lost your father." He shook his head. "We need to let go of all that. Start over, right here, right now. We need to do that for her."

"You really turned out all right, didn't you?"

"Don't go swelling my head, now." He looked at her, then back inside, at Tilda. "I should go."

She nodded. He clasped her hand and leaned down to kiss her again, just as softly and sweetly, but shorter and with a little less certainty. "I promise I'll talk to my father. I'll get to the truth."

The violins in her head stopped playing with an ear-bleed inducing squawk. Her face felt as if it turned to stone, and she said, "I already *told you* the truth."

He blinked at her. "I still have to talk to him. I need to hear his side of the story."

"Fine. Talk to him. If he can come up with some other reason he might've handed my father fifty grand in cash immediately after a discussion about my pregnancy, you let me know. I love a good fairytale."

He blinked, managing to look as confused as if he'd just stepped out his front door and onto planet Mars.

"And then there's the fact that he never told you. My God, Joey, he never told you I was carrying your child."

"I know. Believe me, Em, I know. That's why I need to talk to him. I need answers."

"He doesn't *have* answers. Excuses maybe—"

"I need to hear his side of it, Em. He's my father." He heaved a sigh, seemed about to say something more, then he shook his head and muttered, "I'm gonna go. If you need anything, you call me. Okay?"

She pressed her lips to keep from asking him how he could doubt her word about this and instead just nodded. Then he turned and walked quickly but quietly across the sitting room and out the door. He closed it softly behind him. She barely heard his retreating boot steps, the hall was so thickly carpeted. And that was it. He was gone.

And she was reeling with the knowledge that she'd opened her heart to him, and that he didn't believe her.

∽

Joey had time to think as he walked back to the Long Branch. It was a solid two miles and he was grateful he'd worn his lined denim jacket. Despite the earlier cool winter sunshine, it was chilly tonight. He could see his breath.

Em was angry again. He wasn't even sure why. Did she really think he could *not* talk to his father about this? It would be illogical to expect that, and he was pretty sure she'd realize it once she cooled down and thought about it a little.

She'd always had a temper.

Hell, he was angry, too. If his father had known about Emily's pregnancy and not told him—he just couldn't have. He couldn't have done that.

So he had to get things out in the open between him and Bobby Joe. And then he had to figure out how to feel about that.

Until then, he figured he'd give her some space.

But damn, until she'd got her dander up, things had been…

magic between them. Like going back in time. No, like bringing time forward, bringing the past into the now. It was familiar, so familiar, but also new. Different. The feelings between them hadn't gone away. They'd evolved.

They were parents now. They'd created a life together.

They'd made Matilda Louise Hawkins.

His thoughts ground to a halt there, and his pace slowed down. "I want her to have my name," he said. "Matilda Louise McIntyre." He smiled, loving the sound of it in the night air, and said it again, louder. "Matilda Louise McIntyre. Now that's a name that was meant to be."

The Christmas tree lights were still gleaming, but the parking lot was all but empty when he walked into the big driveway. Only a handful of vehicles remained, every one belonging to family.

Bobby Joe had come back. He and Vidalia were waiting for him in the Long Branch, and so were his two brothers and sister-in-law Kiley, who sent him a worried smile when he walked into the dining room. They were all sitting around a big table in the back.

"There he is," Vidalia said, getting to her feet. "Your father has some explaining to do, Joseph." Then she nodded to Kiley.

Kiley got up too, and then both came toward him. Vi patted his shoulder. Kiley gave him a hug and then they went into the barroom.

Joey stiffened his spine, bracing himself inwardly for the discussion to come, and strode to the table where his father was sitting. Bobby Joe was a handsome man. Rugged face and dark hair, heavy brows and a laugh that was infectious. But he wasn't laughing tonight or even smiling. He was morose. And he ought to be.

His brothers had inherited their father's bone structure, and a softer version of his coloring.

"Rob and I want to stay for this, Joe," Jason said. "I think it's a family thing. But it's a you-thing first, so it's up to you."

"You can stay." Joe pulled out a chair and sat down. He was searching his father's face across the table from him, sort of pleading from inside his own chest for him to say it wasn't true. That Emily was wrong. But Bobby Joe couldn't quite look him in the eye. His hands were on the table, one set of fingers kneading the other. His gaze bounced around the red checkered tablecloth to the glasses in front of each of them.

Joey's was clean and empty with a pitcher of beer beside it. He filled it up, took a sip, swallowed. "Dad?"

Bobby Joe's eyes met his. He said, "I made a bad decision, and it's haunted me ever since, son. But I'm gonna tell you everything. All I ask is that you hear me out."

Another sip, a longer one. Joey set the mug down and nodded. "That's what I'm here for. If you hadn't come back, I'd have come to find you. So go ahead. And this time, don't leave anything out."

He nodded slow, clearly tormented. "Henry came to me. He told me you had got his daughter pregnant. Went on and on about how she was a genius and how her whole brilliant future could be ruined."

"She *is* a genius. We always knew that," Joey said.

Jason nodded. Robby picked up his glass to punctuate the statement with an unspoken *hear, hear*!

"I tried to calm him down," Bobby Joe went on. "I assured him we'd do whatever it took to take care of Emily and the baby, that no son of mine would shirk his responsibilities, and so on. He said no, that she'd decided..." He lowered his head, closed his eyes. "That she'd decided to end the pregnancy." A long sigh erupted from deep inside him. "I said she ought to talk to you first, and he said it was her decision to make and she'd made it. She was at the clinic already, and afterward would be going back to college. There was nothing you could do to change her mind."

"That wasn't true, though," Joey said. "Emily never had any intention of...that."

"That's pretty obvious now, son, but it wasn't then." Bobby Joe shook his head sadly. "I believed him, believed it was a done deal. I knew it would break your heart, Joe. I couldn't bring myself to tell you when you couldn't do anything about it."

Joey heard his father, but he heard his own anger louder. "I had a right to know."

"I know you did. I know you did. But Henry died that very night, and Emily was gone. She just up and left, and I just....." He shook his head. "I made a mistake and I'm sorry."

Joe took a long, slow pull from his glass, set it down, and sought his brothers' eyes. He saw sympathy and support there. Bobby Joe had been wrong in what he'd done and they both knew it.

Setting the glass down, Joe got to his feet again, too full of anger and frustration to sit still. "What about the money, Dad?"

"Money?" Jason blurted. He and Rob both looked from him to their father, clearly stunned.

Bobby Joe pressed his lips tight, shaking his head rapidly. "A shakedown is what that was. All those years working for us. I was *good* to Henry. Paid him more than was even reasonable."

"You said you'd tell me everything. So tell me why Henry had fifty grand in cash that he said came from you."

Bobby Joe nodded. "Henry went off about how his daughter deserved recompense. Recompense, that's what he said. Probably the first time he'd used that word in his life. I was furious. It was obvious he was using the pregnancy to wheedle money out of us. But I wrote him a check. I also told him I'd give him a month to find another job." He lowered his head. "He died that night. Not before he'd cashed the check, though. He must've gone from my office straight to the bank, the ungrateful...." He bit his lip. His heavy shoulders rose and fell tiredly. "When Emily took off without a word, I assumed she'd taken the money and gone back to school like her father told me she'd planned to do."

He got up and came around the table. Joey waited as his father approached. When they stood toe to toe, Bobby Joe looked him right in the eyes, and said, "That's the truth, Joseph. I swear it on my love for Vidalia. That's the truth. And I have been sorry for keeping it from you every single day since. It just...it got to where it was easier to just let it go."

Joey stared right back. It felt as if his chest was on fire. "You cost me three and half years with my daughter. And she might not have another year left."

Jason's chair scraped the floor as he got up, too. "Don't be thinking that way."

Bobby Joe said, "I know what Emily thinks I did. That the money was a payoff. I would never pay a woman to abort my own flesh and blood, and I think you know it."

Shaking his head, Joey backed away, turned and headed toward the stairs and up them. As he slammed into his room and locked the door, he knew, even through the haze of anger and regret and the sense of injustice, that he wasn't going to gut the second floor of the Long Branch. He wasn't going to turn it into one big bachelor's paradise.

He was going to build a house with a big play yard and a bedroom fit for a princess. He knew that with sudden, blinding clarity.

What he didn't know was how he was ever going to forgive his father.

CHAPTER EIGHT

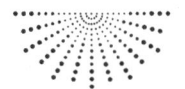

*E*mily dreamed she was home again. She'd finished another year of college, of striving and working and being younger than everyone else at school and trying to live up to her father's expectations.

He'd never gone to college. Neither had her mother. But she was a genius, according to her test scores. And her father's every hope was riding on her small shoulders.

But coming home that summer, she almost didn't want to go back. The little white cottage was so beloved and so familiar. The green lawn and all the pockets of color her father tended so lovingly. He was groundskeeper for the wealthiest family she knew, after all. He was very good at what he did. A genius in his own right, though he couldn't seem to hear that when she said it to him.

That summer. God, it had been so good.

In an instant, she was back there, sneaking over the fence out behind the McIntyre's sprawling mansion, onto the short, green grass her father kept groomed to perfection. She could feel it, cool on her bare feet, and hear the other girls giggling. Her old high school friends, Britt and Taffy and Sue. They all wore bikinis and carried towels and wine coolers as they tiptoed through the darkest part of the McIntyre's lawn, stepping carefully to avoid the sprinklers. She knew where the motion-activated outdoor lights were and guided them around those areas.

She smelled the chlorinated water before they got close enough to see it. It was lit from beneath with soft white lights along the bottom. They made the water seem even more crystalline blue, like an aquamarine. The area around it was tiled, tiny ceramic squares, also blue with darker blue to create patterns and swirls.

Strategically placed palm trees flanked a poolside bar. A towel warmer stood beside it, plugged in 24/7. They slipped silently into the water, her girlfriends, and immediately started splashing and laughing, their voices high pitched and squeaky.

"Shhh! We'll get caught."

They didn't even seem to hear her. Sighing, she sank onto one of the lawn chairs, cracked a wine cooler, drank it. She wasn't in the mood for swimming. She wasn't in the mood for them.

She wanted Joey. She was in love with him. She knew she was. And he was in love with her, too.

And then the dream shifted, and she was in her home, later that same summer, seeing the disappointment, the utter devastation in her father's eyes as she told him what she'd been dreading telling him.

"I'm pregnant, Daddy."

He'd been very still for a long moment, just a slight twitch in his jaw. So strong, her father. Short in stature but stocky and powerful. And his first question had been a predictable one. "Who?"

"Joey McIntyre," she said.

His face had darkened, and it seemed a black cloud moved

behind his eyes. "That spoiled little shit. He's a player. How could you fall for his—"

"It wasn't like that. We...we're in love, Daddy."

"Love?" He'd rolled his eyes. "Do you know how many girls he's seduced, just this year alone? His brothers joke that he's trying to set some kind of a record. He's no good, Emily. What do you think he's going to do when you tell him, eh? You think he's going to marry you or something?"

She blinked, stunned by the venom in her father's tone. "I thought you liked the McIntyres."

"Like them? I work for them. I have to get along. I don't *like* them. They're rich, Emily, and the rich are not to be trusted."

"You're wrong. Joey's different." She shook her head so hard she hurt her neck. "I shouldn't have told you. I should have talked to him first."

"Why didn't you? If you're so sure he will do the right thing by you, why didn't you, Emily?"

She lowered her eyes. "You're upset—"

"Upset? I am devastated. You have a future, a career ahead of you, a plan for your life, daughter. How can you throw that all away over a summer fling with a rich playboy who values you less than a common whore?"

"I'm not a whore!"

"But you acted like one. And you let him treat you like one." He lowered his head, shook it slowly. "I have to go to work." He closed his eyes, then opened them again and, moving closer, ran a hand over her hair, smoothing it back from her face. "Don't do anything yet. Give me some time to process this. I promise you, I'll take care of everything. When I come home, we'll talk again. We'll figure out what to do together, all right?"

He walked away.

Someone was tickling her face, and Emily opened her eyes to see her precious angel grinning down at her and wiggling her fingers on her cheeks. "Mornin', Mommy."

"Morning, Matilda."

"Is it breakfast time?"

She noticed then, the smell of bacon and fresh coffee floating on the air. "It sure smells like it. Let's hurry, huh?"

"Okay!" She bounded out of bed, and Emily had little choice but to follow. And yet the dream stayed with her. That summer. That beautiful, hot, passionate summer she'd spent madly in love with Joey McIntyre. The crushing disappointment she'd felt when her father had handed her a pile of money and told her everyone agreed it would be best...

Her heart had been completely demolished.

Maybe by a lie. Maybe by two old men playing games with the lives of their children. And not even asking what those children wanted or needed. Just making decisions, moving pieces around on a chessboard.

Breakfast smelled so good they decided to eat in their jammies. Emily pulled a pretty pink robe with a ruffled edge around her and shoved her feet into matching slippers. Tilda wore her own perfectly matching ones. She loved being "twins" with her mamma. Each set had come with a pink headband that had a big purple flower attached, and Tilda insisted they wear them as well.

They headed down the stairs, and started for the sunroom where breakfast was usually served, only to stop short when they saw Joey carrying a tray full of food from the kitchen through the huge dining room toward the double doors.

"Oh, good, you're up! Can you open the doors, for me, princess?"

Emily stood there blinking at him. He noticed, and then looked her up and down and smiled while Tilda ran ahead to open the doors.

Ida Mae came from the kitchen behind him, that giant silver coffee pot on its matching tray with all the fixings. She stopped, eyeing Emily, then Joey. "Um, he was insistent on making breakfast for you girls this morning," she explained, correctly reading Emily's expression as less than overjoyed. "I'm sorry if it's not all right."

"It's not," she said. And she said it flatly but quietly, so Matilda wouldn't hear and get upset. "The last thing I want is company before I've even had coffee or a shower."

"Put the food down and go, Joseph," Ida Mae said. "I'm very sorry, Emily, believe me I don't usually—"

"But I *cooked*." Joey looked like a puppy who'd been unexpectedly kicked.

"Come on, Daddy, this door's heavy."

He sent her Tilda grin, then looked at Emily again. "I'm sorry. It's not Ida Mae's fault. I bulled my way into her kitchen. I'll be out of here in ten minutes, okay?"

"No. It's not okay. You're overstepping."

He nodded hard. "You're right. I'm sorry. I'm...I guess I'm trying too hard to make up for lost time. I could hardly bring myself to leave here last night."

"Daddy!"

"I'll just put the food down and go," he whispered, and he hurried through the door Tilda was struggling to hold open, and then set the tray down on one table and started unloading it onto another.

Emily sighed, shook her head, and looked at Ida Mae.

"He really was kind of insistent," she said.

"He's insistent. I'm a paying customer." She softened. "He can't just come around any time he feels like it, all right? This is...a complicated situation."

"Understood. I didn't know...you know, where things were between you."

Em took the coffee tray from her, then turned and carried it out. Ida Mae headed right back into the kitchen, and Emily felt a little bad for being upset with her, but for heaven's sake.

In the sunroom, Joey was placing a plate of food in front of

Tilda. Then he took the cloth napkin, shook it free of its folds, and laid it over her lap like a waiter in a fancy restaurant.

When he saw Em, he moved fast to pull out her chair.

Scowling, she walked past him and set the coffee tray beside the breakfast tray on the second table. As she did, she noticed that the tray he'd brought out had three breakfast plates, not two. Hell.

She turned over one of the two coffee cups and filled it. And then, sighing, she turned over the other and filled that, too. She added cream and sugar to her own and went to the chair. Joey was still standing behind it, one hand on its back. He pulled the chair out for her as she sat down, and then whisked her plate from the tray and set it in front of her.

Bacon, perfectly cooked eggs, their yolks sunny and soft, a thick slice of toast with butter already melted over it. "Looks delicious," she said.

"It *is* delicious. I make a mean breakfast." He glanced at her, at the coffee cup she'd filled for him, then back at her, his eyes asking the question.

"Pull up a chair, Joey. I can't send you packing without even letting you eat, after all this. But next time, ask me first?"

"Absolutely," he said. He grabbed his own plate and coffee, and sat down at the table. "I wanted to ask you about something, and I couldn't wait."

"Maybe you can wait at least until after breakfast, though," she said, with a meaningful glance Tilda's way. No doubt his request had to do with her daughter, and she wasn't going to let him put her on the spot in front of her.

"Oh, sure. Yeah, it can wait that long." He looked chastened, but quickly cheered up again and dug into his food.

She did too, and it was delicious.

Ida Mae came out after they'd all but cleaned their plates and said, "I have some cinnamon buns fresh out of the oven, but um, I need some help putting the icing on."

"Me, me! I can help!" Tilda jumped out of her chair, her plate clean as a whistle. "Can I, Mommy?" she asked, almost as an afterthought, and then she added quickly, "You won't leave, will you Daddy?"

"I won't leave," he promised.

"Go ahead, Tilda. But try to get more icing on the buns than in your belly, okay?"

She giggled and took Ida Mae's hand, skipping beside her back into the house.

Then Emily took her coffee mug and leaned back in her chair. "So?"

He nodded, looking at her. "I should've called first. I'll call first from now on. I was…excited."

"Excited?"

"Rob and Kiley are having a kids' day over at Holiday Ranch. I only just realized it's coming right up. Parents pay ten bucks apiece, and the kids get a hayride, cookies and hot cocoa, and they get to make an ornament for their parents for Christmas. All the local kids are going. Kara and Jimmy will be there with Tyler. Maya and Caleb with the twins."

She said, "And your father?"

He lowered his head. "I don't know if he'll be there or not."

"Then I don't know if Tilda will."

He took a breath, started to speak, then stopped himself and started again. "I talked to him last night."

"And?"

"He admitted he knew you were pregnant and didn't tell me." He sighed. "And I'm furious with him about it, but if you look at it objectively, you did the same thing."

"He tried to pay me to abort his granddaughter."

"No. That's not how he tells it."

Emily leaned forward in her seat. "Really. This, I've gotta hear. How *does* he tell it?"

He pressed his lips together, looked at her and said, "You're not gonna like it."

"I already don't like it. So go on, tell me."

"He says your father told him you'd already decided and were at the clinic. He said there was no changing your mind, that it was too late anyway. And then he suggested that you ought to be paid for all the trouble. It pissed my father off, but he wrote a check anyway. And then he fired him. Gave him a month to find another job."

She listened and got madder with every word. "So your father's the long-suffering billionaire, taken advantage of by his own longtime employee. And my father's the opportunistic money grubber."

"I'm just telling you what Dad told me."

"And you believe him?"

Joey sighed, seemed to search himself, and then nodded. "I have to say, I do. I can't imagine my father trying to pay someone to do that. His own grandchild."

"And you think my father would try to make his own daughter do that to *his* own grandchild?"

"You were his only daughter, Em. He'd been planning your brilliant future since you learned to walk. The pregnancy might've seemed to him like a great big obstacle to those plans. One that would ruin your life. So yeah, I think he would. I think he did."

She stood up slowly. "I think you should go now."

He stood too. "I'm sorry. I know you loved him, but—"

"Just go."

He sighed, lowered his head. "So Sunday…"

"Get. Out. Now." Tears were burning her eyes, and she was having trouble catching her breath.

"I promised Tilda—"

"Go!"

"Okay, okay. I'll pop into the kitchen to say goodbye." He

started for the doorway, then came back. "I'm sorry. I'm really sorry." He touched her shoulder.

She turned her back to him quickly, tears brimming by then, and she'd be damned if she would let him see them.

"I'll call you later. About Sunday."

And then he was gone.

~

Joey got back to the saloon. The only car there was the orange Dodge Charger with its black racing stripes and pugnacious face. It was the kind of car that seemed to be begging cops to pull it over. Noisier than his truck, too, in a purely you-couldn't-take-me-if-you-wanted-to kind of way. (As opposed to a please-someone-fix-my-engine kind of way.)

The Long Branch was empty, chairs up on top of tables, floors shining clean, bar gleaming. Joe meandered into the kitchen, found the stash of baked goods supplied fresh every other day from Sunny's, and got out a fat blueberry muffin for Dax. He warmed it in the microwave while the coffee brewed, then sliced it open just enough to fit in a pat of butter.

He didn't know how the big guy took his coffee, so he erred on the side of cream and sugar and hoped for the best as he carried it up the stairs and knocked on Dax's door.

Either the zombie apocalypse had begun or that was Dax, moaning inhumanly from the other side.

The door wasn't locked, but he had a key anyway. He opened it up and went inside. Dax was in the bed. Sort of. He was fully clothed and lying face down on top of bedding that he'd apparently wrestled with all night. One pillow was over his head, the other one under his face. It was a miracle he hadn't suffocated.

"Dax, wake up," Joey said softly.

"Don't yell—"

"Dax! Wake up!"

Dax jumped a foot off the bed.

"That was me yelling. See the difference there?" He put the food on the nightstand.

Dax rolled over, then slid up until he was sitting semi-upright, looked at Joe, looked around the room, looked at Joe again. "Am I at the Long Branch?"

"You don't remember?" Joey handed him the coffee mug, and Dax sat up a little straighter to take it, to sip. He winced as if his whole face hurt. And then Joey said, "You drove here, Dax."

He froze halfway through his second sip, lowered the cup but kept his eyes on it. "Are you sure?"

"Your car's in the driveway. You staggered through the batwing doors alone, and started yelling for a bartender."

He closed his eyes and swore.

"The bar was closed for a holiday function, a family thing. There were kids here, Dax. *My* kid was here."

"I'm sorry. I'm… dammit, I'm sorry, Joe." Then frowning, he lifted his head, met Joe's eyes. "You have a kid?"

"Yeah, turns out I do. I've known about her for all of three days, and she's seriously ill. So you can imagine how much fun I'm having, dealing with you right now. This is not okay, Dax. And listen up now, because you need to hear this part. *You* are *not* okay."

Dax stared at the muffin, but Joey didn't think he was looking at it. And his face got kind of odd looking. Surprised, almost. And he said, "I'm not, am I?" He blinked and looked at Joey. "Holy shit, Joe, I'm not okay."

"It's all right, pal. You will be." Joey clapped a hand to his shoulder. "Eat your muffin. Take a shower. Get dressed. Rob needs you with your head on straight. He doesn't have anybody else to advise him. He loves horses, but you know 'em. He needs you, Dax."

He lowered his head. "It's hard bein' around Kiley. She looks so much like…like Kendra. You know?"

"Well they're twins," Joe said. Then he frowned. "We're talking about the same Kendra who conned you out of a pile of money, cost you your job, screwed up your relationship with your father—"

"That was already screwed up." He sighed. "Forget it. It doesn't matter. I'll get outta your hair—"

"I want you to stay. I want to help you kick the booze."

"I'm not gonna kick booze sleeping over a saloon, Joe."

That probably made sense. Joey sighed. "What are you gonna do, then?"

He seemed, for a long time, to be thinking.

Joe said, "I can find you a room somewhere else. Maybe Rob and Kiley.... Just stay for today, give yourself some time to figure out what you need to do. Nobody in this establishment is gonna serve you pal, and if you try to help yourself, I'm here, too. I'll know. And I'll kick your ass."

Dax, who outweighed Joey by fifty pounds, most of it muscle, grinned at him. "Okay, Joe. Thanks." Then he squinted at him a little. "And I'm sorry…your little girl is sick. I hope things work out okay."

"So do I."

He nodded slowly. "Why are you doing this? Helping me like this? We're not even friends."

"I consider that freckle-faced shithead Kiley my sister. And I love her." He shrugged. "She likes you. Any friend of hers is a friend of mine. It's what we do in this family."

"I appreciate it," he said. He extended a hand. "Thank you."

Joe clasped his hand, good and firm. "You're welcome."

∼

Six hours later, Emily stood holding her little girl's hand, in front of a white clapboard cottage with burgundy shutters and window boxes full of weeds. They'd driven all day to get there. Her childhood home.

She'd had to come back. Somewhere in this cottage, there had to be proof, evidence, a clue, about what exactly had happened between her father and Bobby Joe McIntyre that long ago day.

The cottage was part of the McIntyre estate, a mile from the main house at the end of a secluded drive. After her father's death, she'd received a letter from the McIntyres' lawyer, giving her permission to live in the cottage for as long as she wanted. Aside from removing the food from the fridge and cabinets, the family had left the place just as it had been, the letter had said. Nothing would be touched. There were instructions on how she could turn on the power if and when she returned.

She figured all of that was just Bobby Joe's effort to ease his guilty conscience. She'd never written back, just silently vowed she would never set foot in the place again.

But she stood there now, and the sun was going down. There was a hard wind blowing, twigs and leaves skittering.

"Where are we, Mommy?"

"This is where I grew up," she said. "When I was a little girl just like you, I lived right here."

"Wow."

"Come on, let's go in." She held Matilda's hand and went up the walk, then around to the side of the cottage where the power box was. There was a handle. She had to push it up to the ON position. Simple. So she did, and then led Tilda around to the front of the house and unlocked the door.

When she opened it, the past hit her like a tidal wave. Just the smell of the place, though a little musty and stale, was familiar all the same. She closed her eyes and inhaled. Tears burned, and she whispered, "Oh, Daddy..."

"Turn on the lights!"

Emily found the switch without thinking and turned on the

lights. She was standing right where she'd been standing the last time she'd looked at her father. And the ghosts of their final conversation whispered from the corners.

Everyone agrees this will be for the best, Emily. You're not just anyone, you are gifted. You are destined for so much more.

More? More than being a mother to your grandchild? A mother to Joey McIntyre's baby? He really believes that?

We all agree.

Well, I don't agree. And mine is pretty much the only opinion that matters.

Emily, you can't throw your life away.

Just as easily as you can throw your grandchild away. Throw your daughter away. Because that's what you just did.

In her mind, she backed up the movie, just a few frames, and tried to replay it in slo-mo.

"He really believes that?" she heard herself ask her father again.

In her mind, she zoomed in on her father's eyes. The way his eyelids flinched, and his gaze shifted away from hers.

"We all agree."

He'd never said Joey knew. He'd only implied it, and had been unable to look her in the eye while he did.

"Show me around, Mommy."

Em glanced at the sofa and flashed on her father lying sideways across it. That was where she'd found him, hours after their final confrontation.

Heart attack. She'd broken his heart right after he'd broken hers. He and Joey McIntyre had taken sledge hammers to it.

And now she knew that Joey was innocent. They'd never told him. If she'd needed proof, she'd seen it in her father's eyes, when she'd asked him flat out about Joey's part in the discussion. He'd had no part in it. It was obvious now. It should have been obvious then.

She'd have got the truth out of him, if he'd lived. But he'd died and taken his lies to his grave.

Sighing, she led Tilda through the living room to the little bedroom off one side that had been her own. Faded posters of animals still lined the walls. There were a lot of horses. There were cute kittens and puppies and even some piglets. Puffins and hippos and several monkeys. There were miniature animals too, figurines and models, and her bedding and curtains had been wild horse themed. Tilda went to the dressing table, pulled out the wooden stool and climbed up on it. She pawed through items on the stand, and Emily leaned over her, looking on as time fell away.

She flashed back to sitting right where Tilda sat now, brushing her curls and staring into the mirror and dreaming about Joey McIntyre telling her he loved her. He would say it, she just knew he would. How could he look at her the way he did, with those soulful brown eyes, and not love her?

"Will you paint my nails, Mommy?"

She came back to the present, saw Tilda picking up one bottle of nail polish after another. The mirror had a photo of her and Joey on their first day of Kindergarten, standing side by side, backpacks in place. She would have been terrified if Joey hadn't been going, too.

"Who is that, Mommy?" Tilda asked, tugging the photo from the mirror.

"That's Mommy," she said, putting her fingertip on her own image. Then she moved it and said, "And that's your daddy."

"Wow!"

"You look like him, Tilda. Those brown eyes could melt a fudgesicle."

"My hair is like yours."

"It is, isn't it?" Emily asked, stroking her daughter's curls.

They headed back to the kitchen, and Emily put away the few groceries she'd bought on the way and made them soup and sandwiches for supper. Then they played in the back yard before coming in for a bath and a story.

And finally, Tilda was asleep in Emily's childhood bed, and Emily was alone with her memories. It was amazing how strongly the old feelings came back, just as fresh as if they were new again. The zing of being madly in love with a beautiful young man. The way she'd felt before the lie. When she thought he loved her, too.

My God, what if he had?

A very light tap came on the cottage door. Frowning, she went to answer it, and found herself face to face with Joey McIntyre's mother.

Judith hadn't changed at all. Her hair was still long and naturally wavy, and she still wore it shoulder length with a slight side part. The curls were white now, but you couldn't be blamed for mistaking them for platinum blond because her face was so exquisite. The cheekbones were the kicker, and those light blue eyes that still sparkled. She was thinner than Emily remembered. The curves of youth were long gone. She was slender now, and it made her seem taller and more graceful when she moved.

"Hello, Emily," she said softly. "I understand I have a granddaughter."

Emily lowered her head. "She's um...asleep right now."

"Could I just... look at her?" Her voice was so soft, her eyes so hopeful. She didn't seem, in that moment, like a billionaire member of the Texas elite. She seemed almost like a child herself.

"Of course you can. Come in."

She walked into the cottage, looking around as she did. As Em led the way to the bedroom, she spoke softly, feeling awkward and needing to fill the silence with something. "Thank you for keeping the place for me. I was...pretty surprised to see how little had changed."

"I've always considered you a part of my family, Emily."

Em walked into the bedroom, and Judith followed. Then she stood beside the bed, gazing down at her grandchild for a long moment, absolute wonder and awe in her eyes, until a hitch in her breathing made a soft sound. Pressing her hand to her lips, Judith backed silently out of the room and pulled the door closed.

"She's beautiful. She's so beautiful, Em."

"She has Joey's eyes," Em said softly. "I'm really sorry I kept her from you." She thought, even as she'd said the words, that they were nowhere near enough. She'd hurt a lot of people with her decision to run away and keep Tilda's existence a secret.

Judith nodded. "I know why you did it."

"How?" She walked to the kitchen, Judith beside her, and made them each a cup of tea.

"Bobby Joe called right after you arrived in Big Falls," Judith said, taking a seat at the little table. "He told me what he did, all those years ago. And he also told me why he kept it from me. He knew I would tell Joey, and that Joey would be devastated to learn your decision, and he didn't want to put him through that. He believed it was a done deal."

"That's what he told Joey, too." Emily sipped her tea slowly, to gather courage for the rest. "But he gave my father fifty thousand dollars."

"I know. He says your father asked him for it. He was so angry, both over your decision to abort his grandchild and for what he considered your father's betrayal." She sighed. "I know that's really an awful thing to think about your dad, and I don't blame you for not wanting to believe it. But I can only tell you that I know Bobby Joe, and I know when he's lying. And I believe him." Then she added, "And he did fire your father that day. I was furious but he refused to tell me why."

She sipped her tea while Emily digested all of that. Then she said, "I can tell you this, sweetheart. He mourned that baby.

After your father's death, he was inconsolable. I thought it was because Henry had been with us for so long, thought he was grieving. And he was. But now I know it wasn't for Henry. It was for that little girl in there." She smiled through wet eyes as she gazed toward the bedroom door. "Thank goodness his grief was misplaced. Thank God. Thank *you*, Emily."

Emily frowned, because Judith was sincere. Could it really be true? Could her father have demanded the money and told Bobby Joe the abortion was a *fait accompli*?

"How long are you staying, Emily?"

"Just overnight."

Judith's smile was quick and bright. "Will you bring her by the house for breakfast in the morning? Just for an hour or two? Give me a chance to get to know her just little bit before you head back to Big Falls?"

Emily nodded. "Yes. Of course I will. You're her grandmother."

At that word, Judith pressed perfectly manicured fingertips to her lips, and her tears spilled over. "I'm a grandmother," she whispered. "Lord, this is such a gift. A miracle, really."

Emily saw her joy and wondered.... "Did Bobby Joe tell you about her condition?" she asked softly.

Judith nodded. "Yes, he did. Bobby Joe has more money than God, Emily, and I have nearly as much. Tilda's going to get the best medical care there is. I promise."

Judith finished her tea and got to her feet, then leaned down, stroked a hand over Emily's hair, and kissed the top of her head before straightening again. "When I think of you so young, all alone and afraid and pregnant..." She shook her head slowly. "And yet, you had her. You raised her. You finished school. You started your own business." She looked Emily right in the eyes and said, "I'm proud of you, Emily. And my granddaughter is blessed to have you as her mother."

CHAPTER NINE

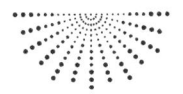

"Where is she?" Joey asked.

He was standing on Ida Mae Peabody's big front porch, talking to the aging innkeeper through her slightly-open door. Emily hadn't been answering her phone all day. He knew he'd ticked her off at breakfast, first by showing up uninvited, and then by defending his father. But when he'd arrived to find her van gone, panic had set in.

What if she wasn't coming back? What if the past few days were all the time he would ever get with his little girl? What if Tilda got sick and he wasn't there to help her?

"I'm not her keeper, Joseph," Ida Mae said. "I don't know where she went, and I wouldn't tell you if I did."

"Well, when did she leave? You can tell me that, can't you?"

"Right after breakfast." Ida Mae bit her lip. "Listen, this is my place of business and she's a guest. I really can't say any more. I won't."

"Did she check out? Did she take her things?"

"I told you, I'm not saying more." She started to close the door.

Joe stuck his foot in it. "Let me in so I can check her room, then."

"No!"

"Ida Mae, she has my little girl." He started to push the door open.

She pulled it wider, surprising him, but then suddenly slammed it on his foot with more strength than a seventy-year-old should have been able to muster. He yipped, held his foot in one hand and hopped.

Locks turned audibly. "Go home, Joseph McIntyre!"

"Dammit, Ida Mae, she took Matilda Louise!" He knocked and knocked again. He poked the doorbell several times. But Ida Mae did not respond in any way.

"Dammit, dammit, dammit." He had known Emily was mad at him, but he hadn't imagined she would take Tilda and run. And now he didn't know what the hell to do.

He tugged out his phone to Call Caleb.

Cal's latest receptionist answered. He'd been through several in the past few months. "Montgomery Law Office. How may we—"

"Put Caleb on. Hurry."

"I'm sorry, but—"

"I'm his cousin-in-law and it's urgent. Put him on the phone." He wasn't being very nice, and he figured he'd regret it later. But right then—

"Joe?" Caleb asked.

"Cal, thank God. Listen she left."

"What? Who left?"

"Emily. She's gone. She's not at the boarding house. Her van is gone. Ida Mae won't tell me where the hell she is or even whether she checked out and—"

"Hey, calm down. Just take a breath and calm dow—"

"I'm *not* going to freakin' calm down, Cal. She's gone and she has my little girl." He was frantic, pacing up and down the sidewalk in front of Ida Mae's and yelling into his phone like some kind of maniac, and he knew it, but was too afraid to be ashamed.

And then an SUV with the Big Falls PD emblem on the side pulled to a stop behind his truck, and his brother-in-law Jimmy Corona got out.

"Shit, Jimmy's here. You might need to come over," he said into his phone. No answer. "Caleb?"

There was no reply, and he looked down at the phone to see the "Call Ended" message on the screen. About a second later, a text popped up from Caleb.

Get away from Ida Mae's NOW. Come to my office if you think you can act like a reasonably sane human being.

Great.

He shoved the phone into his pocket. Jimmy came to him, long easy strides, impressive uniform, whipcord build. "Morning, Joe."

"You here to arrest me?"

"Why? You do something illegal?"

"No. Emily did. She took Tilda somewhere, and I don't know where. I have a court order—"

"I heard you told her to tear that up. Gesture of good will or something like that."

"Yeah, but she left. She took my little girl, Jimmy. My sick little girl."

"I spoke to Ida Mae," Jimmy said. And maybe his slow-bordering-on-lazy tone was supposed to calm him, but it was only making him madder. "Emily didn't check out. She said she'd be back tomorrow."

"Why the hell couldn't Ida Mae have just told me that?"

"Maybe cause it's none of your business?"

"It's totally my business. And it could be a lie. It would give her plenty of time to take Tilda even farther away from me before I realize—"

"Where? You think she's gonna take a sick toddler to Mexico? You've gotta learn to have a little faith. Now, Ida Mae says you're scaring her. I thought she was overreacting, but now that I see how worked up you are... You need to leave. Go home, Joe."

"I can't just go home and wait while she takes my daughter God knows where! She's sick. I've already lost three years of her life, dammit, I'm not gonna lose any more."

Jimmy took a deep breath. "So you're refusing to leave?"

"I'm gonna stay right here until she brings my little girl back."

Lowering his head, Jimmy muttered, "Damn you for all the grief I'm gonna get from the family for this. Turn around, Joe."

"What?"

"Turn your stubborn ass around." Jimmy didn't wait this time, but grabbed hold of Joey's wrist, snapped a handcuff on it, and spun him around. He had the other hand cuffed behind his back before Joey even knew what was happening.

"You're *arresting* me?"

"What did you think I was gonna do? You didn't give me a choice. Get in the damn car, back seat, and keep your mouth closed until Caleb shows up, you love-sick dumbass."

Joey sighed and stomped to the SUV, got into the back. "You're just giving her time to take Tilda farther away, Jim. You're family."

Jimmy closed his door, got behind the wheel and drove. "I'm the police chief, too. And while I may bend the rules for my own from time to time, I'm not gonna let you harass a sweet old lady into a heart attack."

"Come on, Ida Mae knows I'd never hurt a fly."

"Then why do you s'pose she felt the need to call 911?" He turned the corner onto Main Street, and drove above the 30 mph speed limit.

Joe slammed his head back against the seat rest, closed his

eyes, knew he'd been acting like an idiot. "You're right. I'm chastised."

"Yeah, well, you're gonna spend an hour or two in a cell, bro, until Ida Mae decides not to press charges."

"What if she doesn't?"

Jimmy pulled over in front of the police department, got out, and opened Joey's door for him. "If she doesn't, then you're gonna be charged with misdemeanor trespass, face a judge, and probably end up paying a fine. It's not the end of the world."

"It is if she gets out of the country with my kid."

~

Joey was out of jail by dinner time. Ida Mae declined to press charges, but she did ask Jimmy to tell him that he needed to learn some manners. After that, Joe didn't much know what to do with himself.

Sophie had called to say she now had blood from every member of the family, and that it had all been delivered to a nearby lab for testing. She went on about how it was more complicated than just typing the blood. The human leukocyte antigen had to match. The reminder of this dormant illness crouching inside his little girl, waiting to strike at any time, made him too sick to eat. He paced, and his stomach was all out of whack.

His father had come by, told him Emily and Tilda were in Texas. They'd spent the night at the cottage and the morning with his mother, and would be back later in the evening. He wasn't sure whether to trust that or not. Maybe Emily was in Texas, but that didn't guarantee she'd be back.

He was riding herd on a full house at the Long Branch and trying to keep himself distracted from worrying when Emily walked through the batwing doors. He saw her before she saw him. Snug fitting jeans, a pretty green blouse that seemed silky and sexy without being low cut or clingy. She looked around the place and then spotted him behind the bar.

Jason saw her, too, and put a hand on Joe's shoulder. "Go ahead, I've got this. And Joe, be *nice*, all right?"

He came out from behind the bar and met her near the doors. She said nothing, just turned and walked outside, away from the din of crowd, the holiday music, the lights, all of it, assuming he'd follow.

He did, stepping out into the sudden silence of the night. It was cold. The parking lot was packed with cars gleaming beneath the overhead lights. His breath made clouds and so did hers. She was wearing a jacket. He wasn't.

"I hear you've had an adventurous day," she said.

He rolled his eyes. Sometimes he hated the family grapevine. "Stressful day. Like you might have if I took off with Tilda and didn't even tell you I was going, much less where or when I'd be back."

She was quiet for a moment, then said, "I needed some time. And if you trusted me, you'd have been okay giving me some."

"Trust you? You've kept her from me her whole life, and now you want me to trust you not to try to take her from me again?"

"I can't take her from you, because you don't have her."

"I'm her father."

"I'm her mother. And the only family she's ever known."

"And whose fault is that?" He pushed a hand through his hair, looked around and spotted the van. "Where is she now?"

"Sleeping. Ida Mae's keeping an eye on her until I get back."

"So you'll leave her with Ida Mae, but not with me?"

She closed her eyes. "She's sleeping. I'm going right back."

"I have rights, Emily." He met her eyes, saw the fear that came into them, shook his head at how deeply it hit him and how easily he read it.

"I thought we agreed to put off fighting over her until she's well."

"Yeah, well that's not gonna work if you can't respect my rights to my child."

She set her jaw. "She's been mine and mine alone for years, Joe. I'm not used to having to get anyone's permission to take my daughter on an overnight road trip."

"You'd better *get* used to it, because if this happens again—"

"What? You gonna tape your court order back together and take me to face some local judge who's probably a relative of yours like everyone else in this town?" Angry tears welled up in her eyes.

He took a deep breath. "No." Heaving a heavy sigh, he looked at the ground, at the toes of his boots. "I'm pissed, okay? You scared the hell out of me and I'm pissed."

"I will never ask your permission to do what I want with my child."

He pressed his lips tight. "For now," he said, "I will settle for notification. Is that too much to ask? That you just let me know when you plan to leave town, where you're going, when you're coming back?"

"Yeah. It is."

He lowered his head and paced away. She was being unreasonable. He supposed he had been, too. She'd made him angry. He'd made her angry right back. It wasn't going to help Tilda. "Do you know how much it hurts me that you're here, and she's back at the house with Ida Mae, a woman you've known less than a week? But you won't trust her with me? Do you know how that feels?"

He came back to her, looked her in the eyes. "You loved me once, Emily."

"So what?"

He narrowed his eyes. She was flushing, her cheeks reddening. Might be anger, might be memory. "You admitted you did me wrong by keeping her from me all these years. But you keep right on compounding the wrong. Repeating it. Acting like I've got no say in anything. She's my *daughter*, Em. Try to put yourself in my shoes. What if I took her and kept her from you for the next three years? Huh? How would that feel?"

"It's not the same. You never knew she existed. You weren't aching for her all that time, like I'd be."

"No. I'm just aching now for the time that you stole from me. Time I'll never get back. Honestly, I'm not sure I can ever forgive you for that."

That brought her to silence. He stared into her eyes a long moment, saw that maybe he was getting through to her, so he pressed his luck. "You're not the only one whose heart got broken back then, Emily. I was in love with you, and you just up and vanished. Sent me a postcard. A fucking postcard. I didn't get over it for months." He lowered his head, and his voice hoarse, he added, "That's a lie. The truth is, I never got over it."

And then he just turned and went back into the saloon.

∽

Joey was right, dammit. Emily knew he was right, and yet she couldn't bring herself to admit it. Why hadn't she just admitted her mistake in not telling him her plans and apologized?

Because she resented having to share Matilda with anyone. Anyone. And now she was being forced to share her with a whole pile of people all at once. Strangers. She didn't know them and she didn't trust them and she didn't particularly want to.

She sat on the front porch swing. Ida Mae had long since gone to bed. Tilda was still sleeping soundly. Emily had the baby monitor receiver beside her on the swing, and was rocking slowly back and forth.

It was almost midnight.

Someone came walking up the street. His long strides and

easy gait were familiar. Even in silhouette, she recognized Joey. Hands shoved into his pockets, head down, walking along.

She watched him coming, stayed where she was until he got right up to the Peabody's Boarding House sign. The porch was in shadow, and she'd stilled the swing. He paused there, looking up at her window. A big fat tear rolled down his cheek, and her heart clenched up in her chest. Then sighing, he lowered his head, turned and started walking back the way he'd come.

She got up from the swing and ran down the steps. He heard her, and turned, and when she got to him, she wrapped her arms around his neck, and pressed her mouth to his. He got over his shock in a hurry, hugged her waist and bent over her, cupping the back of her head, feeding from her mouth, bending her backwards, kissing her deeply.

And then he lifted his head, looking down into her eyes.

"I'm sorry!" They both blurted it at the same instant.

She smiled, tears burning down her face. "It wasn't a big a deal. I should have told you. I was mad that you didn't take my word for what happened, that you were still protecting your father."

"I should've trusted you. You said you wouldn't take her from me—"

"I'll let you take her to the Holiday Ranch tomorrow," she said.

"You can come, too."

"I don't have to. I need to...I need to let go a little bit. You're her father."

He nodded. "I want you to come."

She nodded, the movements jerky, the tears still flowing. "Okay."

"Okay."

CHAPTER TEN

*I*n the secluded clearing near the falls for which their town was named, Selene Brand Falconer stood with her best friends. She'd met her husband Cory in this very spot, when he'd stumbled out of the woods, wounded and bleeding, and had literally fallen at her feet.

Not much had changed. The sound of the rushing waterfall still provided the perfect background music for magic. The stars twinkled from the wide, endless expanse of sky. It was chilly tonight. You could see your breath.

There was a big boulder in the center of their clearing now. It had been along the edge of the falls for centuries, but the women had teamed up to roll it a few yards—a monumental task, but worth it. It made the perfect altar. It held the usual items: a censer, wafting sandalwood smoke into the night, an onyx cup full of blessed water, a ritual dagger known as an *athame* with sacred symbols carved into its handle, a hollowed-out piece of quartz filled with sea salt, and a tiny cauldron in the center, just big enough to contain its tea light candle.

And one item that wasn't usually there. A photo of Matilda

Louise Hawkins, soon to be Matilda Louise McIntyre, if Selene's senses were true to form.

The women stood in a circle around the center stone. Selene in the west, as always. Her affinity for the moon goddess who shared her name and her moonspun hair made her feel aligned with those energies.

Helena, in the East, was the first to speak. Her brunette waves moved softly in the breeze she invoked as she lifted her hands. "I call on the energies of the east, of air, and thought, and motion. And of healing. Lend thy power unto our spell."

Marcy stood in the south, flame-haired and fiery, she was a powerful conjurer. She raised her hands just as Helena had. "I call on the energies of the south, of fire and passion and action. And of healing. Lend thy power unto our spell."

Selene raised her hands toward the west. "I call on the energies of the west, of the moon and the sea, of transformation. And of healing. Lend thy power unto our spell." She felt the energy fill her and imagined handing off to Erica in the North.

The north used to be Tessa's spot, but since her death, the others had opted to keep her in the center. Her personal book of shadows represented her there. It stood on the ground, propped against the boulder. They never held a ritual without Tessa's book there.

Erica fit in the north. She was strong and reliable, steady and powerful. She'd toned down her goth look a lot since they'd first started meeting. Instead of jet black, her hair was dark brown, her makeup far less dramatic than in the past.

"I call on the energies of the north," she intoned. "Of earth, and strength and manifestation. And of healing. Lend thy power unto our spell."

When she felt the energy had filled her, she nodded once, and all four of them turned to face the center and spoke as one. "We call on the energies of the center, of the great above and the ascended ones. And of healing. Of the great below and our beloved ancestors. And of healing. Lend thy power unto our spell."

And then, moving closer to the boulder, Selene lit the two candles that stood there, one for the Goddess and one for the God, and they each closed their eyes to silently ask for the Divine to join them in their circle.

Once she felt their powerful presence, Selene faced her sister Witches, and said, "We're working tonight for the healing of Matilda Louise, if that be in keeping with her soul's purpose in this lifetime. We want her whole. We want her well. We want her happy. We want her strong. We want her to enjoy a lifetime that's rich and long."

Nodding, Marcy said, "Whole and well. Happy and strong. Enjoy a lifetime rich and long." And then she said it again, clapping her hands to create a rhythm. "Whole and well. Happy and strong. Enjoy a lifetime rich long."

Erica picked up her drum, slung the strap over her shoulder and began beating out an elaborate rhythm that fit perfectly. Helena grabbed a rattle, shaking it in time, and they began moving clockwise around the circle, repeating the chant over and over. Their steps became a dance, arms rising, swirling, hips moving, feet keeping time. The drumbeat increased in tempo and their movements followed pace. The chant grew louder and more urgent. Higher and higher the energy grew.

Selene could all but see it, a swirling, inverted vortex of magic, rising from their circle to a point far above it. The cone of power. They fed it with their energy, their words, their dancing footsteps, until the energy was vibrating so high and so strong they could not doubt its existence.

The chant was rapid now. "Whole-well-happy-strong. Make her lifetime rich and long. Whole-well-happy-strong. Make her lifetime rich and long. *Wholewellhappystrong! Makeherlifetimerichand LONG!*"

They stopped all at once, without even a signal. The power

was so strong, so clear, and they'd been working together for so long, they could sense when the energy had peaked and it was time to release it. As they let the power rush out of them, Selene focused on Tilda's photo, willing all that healing to go directly to the little girl it represented. As they let the magic fly, they went almost limp and sank to the ground as one.

At the very same moment, Tessa's book of Shadows, propped against the base of the center stone like it always was, fell face-first onto the ground.

The women all looked at each other, their eyes wide. Selene whispered, "Thanks, Tessa. We need all the help we can get on this one." And she blew a kiss skyward.

Gradually, they rose, bid thanks and farewell to all the energies they had invoked and closed the circle. But the entire time, the buzz of magic remained in Selene's veins. It had felt different tonight, more powerful than any ritual they had ever attempted.

"It's going to be okay," she whispered. "Somehow, it's going to be okay."

~

The arching HOLIDAY RANCH sign over the driveway was trimmed in white edged holly leaves, and dotted with heavy bunches of bright red berries. Silver bells, big ones, marked the arch's center, long weighted ribbons dangling from their clappers. Crystal snowflakes hung from the end of each ribbon, catching the breeze, so the bells were ringing constantly.

And that was just the beginning. The place could've been called North Pole, Oklahoma. There was a playground area, with white sand and igloo-shaped playhouses made of plastic and wood. A hay wagon that looked like a sleigh was pulled behind a pair of horses with jingle bell harnesses and glittery garland. Teens and adults wore green elf hats to identify them as employees.

Emily looked down at her little girl. Tilda was looking around, wide eyed. She wore her new fuzzy green hat, because it was chilly today, and she'd been begging to wear it ever since she'd got it. Kiley met them halfway between the parking area and the small barn that had been transformed into Santa's workshop. Spray-on snow clung to each windowpane. Christmas music wafted from speakers mounted above the open barn doors.

"This is amazing," Emily said.

Joe's sister-in-law Kiley was beaming with pride. Her eyes were sparkling, and her smile was infectious. "I can't believe how many people are coming! I've sold like a hundred ornaments already today." She crouched lower and said, "Hi, Tilda! Welcome to Holiday Ranch. I'm so glad you could come." Then she offered her an elf hat made of felt. Red, not green like the staff wore.

"Thanks!" Tilda pulled off the new winter hat she'd begged to wear, and handed it to Emily, then allowed Kiley to put the elf hat on her.

"You're welcome. Every kid gets one. And a Hayride-Sleighride, and a cup of hot cocoa, and if you want to, you can make an ornament in the workshop to take home."

Emily wondered how the ranch turned a profit, giving so much away, but looking around, she saw clearly how it was possible. The kids got things free for their $10 admission fee, but the parents were all carrying shopping bags and sipping cocoa too. And a lot of them were eating baked goods, as well.

Kiley was walking while she was talking, taking them through the wide-open barn door into her "workshop." "Everything in that section over there is made by local artists and crafters. We sell them here at a little markup."

There were candles, wood sculptures, jewelry, pottery, hand-painted signs, dolls, potpourri, potholders...

"This is one creative town," Emily said.

"Who knew, right? The edible goodies are on that side. Free cocoa for the kids. Coffee for the grownups. Cider too. And plenty of cookies and treats from Sunny's. Again, we take a markup." She nodded toward the back wall, which was lined, floor to ceiling, with ornaments, glittering, sparkling, gleaming. And strings crisscrossed every available bit of ceiling space, holding wreath after wreath after wreath. The place smelled of cinnamon and pine.

"I wanna ride the horsey!" Tilda shouted as she caught a glimpse of the horses grazing in a distant pasture, out past the larger barn.

"Then the horsey, you shall ride." Joey had just come up behind them. He scooped Tilda up and she squealed in surprise. "I'm glad you came!"

"Me, too."

He met Emily's eyes over their little girl's head, and she nodded hello, then went over to him. Tilda headed to the craft table where piles of safe, plastic ornaments waited to be decorated with paints and glitter, and Kiley went behind her.

Emily didn't go after her, because she was in plain sight. She was a nervous wreck about doing what she was about to do. Taking a deep breath, she said, "I'm going to leave her with you for an hour."

He lifted his brows up so high his elf hat tilted backwards. "You are?"

"If it's okay with you."

"Of course it is." He frowned at her. "Did pigs grow wings or has hell frozen over?"

She made a face at his swear word, casting a quick glance around and seeing there were no little ones within earshot. "Ida

Mae's friend Betty Lou has a sick dog. She asked me to take a look. Just called me on the way here."

"Not going to argue, but didn't you tell her you were taking time off to deal with Tilda's illness?"

"She doesn't know about that."

"Honey, everyone in town knows."

She looked around, noticing the looks being sent her way by all who passed. Kind eyes, sympathetic ones, worried ones, encouraging ones.

"Not that I'm arguing against it. Knowing Ida Mae, I doubt she'd ask if she didn't think it was serious."

Em eyed Tilda, gnawing on her lip. "It shouldn't take long."

"I've got this," he said. "Promise. Go ahead. I won't take my eyes off her."

She looked at him, looked at Tilda again, nodded. "It's hard, leaving her."

"Did you take her on all your calls back in New Mexico?"

"No. But I had a daycare person I trusted—not that I don't trust you," she added quickly. "I just…it's new," she finished, and it was lame and she knew it.

"Go ahead. She'll be okay."

She nodded and went to the craft table. Tilda had chosen an ornament shaped like a woman's shoe, and was gluing tiny multicolored plastic jewels all over its heel. "Mommy's going to go take care of a sick dog. You're going to stay here with your dad and have fun, and I'll be back in a little while. Okay?"

"Kay."

She never even looked up, her focus on her task. Her little tongue was poking out in concentration.

"Can I have a hug goodbye?"

"How 'bout a cheek kiss?" Tilda asked, eyes on the shoe, but tipping her cheek up.

"Grrr." Emily bent and kissed her cheek, then wrapped her up in a big hug anyway. "You be good."

"I will."

Nodding, she straightened and turned to Joey. He was watching her, and there was a light in his eyes that touched her. He was happy, grateful, and directing all of it her way.

"She's fast, Joey," Em said. "She can be there and then gone in as long as it takes you to blink."

"I've got it. I promise. Go, heal the sick puppy. I'll see you when you get back."

∼

It was, he thought, the best hour of his life. Right up there on the same level with the first time he and Emily had made love on the soft green grass, concealed by fragrant blossoms in the poolside garden, long ago. He had his little girl all to himself. He helped her decorate her ornament, and let her pick out a wreath to hang on her bedroom door. He carried her around on his shoulders, and played with her in the play yard, and they took a hot cocoa break together when they got tired out.

He'd never thought all that much about fatherhood. But looking down at that little girl with her mother's burnished curls and his own brown eyes, seeing the absolute love in those eyes when they gazed up at him, brought him feelings he'd never known. This was a whole new thing, a powerful thing.

They were on the Hayride-Sleighride, laughing and singing "Jingle Bells" with a bunch of other kids and parents. He was sitting in the hay, his hands at Tilda's waist and she was standing, so she could see over the elaborately painted plywood sleigh cutouts attached to the sides, to see the rushing Cimarron river beside them. The path they took wound thrillingly close to the river's edge.

And then something happened. There was a huge bang, the wagon dropped sharply to the right. Joe was slammed to one side, cracking his head hard, and Tilda was gone. Just gone. Kids were crying, parents were picking them up, brushing them off.

He sprang to his feet, frantically searching the wagon. "Tilda!"

She shrieked from too far away and his heart froze as he spotted her. She was in the river!

And within another second, he was too.

Panic was as icy cold in his veins as the river water was on his skin as he plunged in. Memories of being under the water, tangled in seaweed, unable to get up, running out of air, came rushing back, but his fear for Tilda was stronger, louder, and drove him on. He came up sputtering, and swam as best he could, toward where he'd last seen her, trying to keep moving while at the same time trying to spot her again. The current was strong and did most of the work. His flailing arms and kicking feet helped him steer, but no one would've called what he was doing swimming.

Someone shouted, "Sharp left, Joey!" It was Rob's voice.

He obeyed and spotted her, bounding up and down, riding the current downstream and wailing in terror. He paddled toward her with everything he had, and within seconds, she was in his arms and she was hugging his neck so tight he could barley breathe. "I've got you, baby. I've got you. You're okay." He held her head up above the water, and sought the bottom with his feet, but the current was strong and kept knocking them out from beneath him. He took the brunt of it as he slowly made his way to the shore, thirty yards downstream from where he'd gone in. His brother Rob was waist deep by then, reaching out a hand, getting hold of Joey's arm, pulling him up onto the riverbank.

Kiley was waiting there, under a sprawling river birch with a big blanket, and as he staggered toward her with Tilda's face buried in his neck. He realized he didn't feel right. The ground was moving in waves. His legs were unsteady. He was having trouble putting one foot in front of the other.

"Jeeze, Joey—"

"My God what happened!" Emily's shout cut Kiley off. Joe was wrapping his little girl in the big blanket when Emily suddenly tore her from his arms, arranging the blanket herself, holding Tilda, rocking her as she sobbed and shivered. "Are you okay, baby? Are you okay?"

"There was an accident—" Joey began.

"The accident was leaving her with you! What was I thinking? You've never even…"

He wasn't hearing much, and he didn't realize he was falling until he hit the ground.

"Joey!"

He heard that, and Tilda shrieking "Daddy!" Not much else, though.

~

Emily's fury evaporated the instant Joey toppled like a felled redwood. A dark red pool spread into the grass where his head had landed. Tilda started howling and reaching and trying to twist out of Emily's arms. Joey's brother Rob fell to his knees beside him, and gently lifted his head, turning it so he could see where the blood was coming from. She could see, too, and hoped she'd covered Tilda's eyes before she had. There was a gash in the back of Joe's skull that looked like it had been made by an axe. She sucked in a breath, staggering backwards.

Rob looked up and said, "Get Sophie."

"She's already on her way," Kiley said. Then she shot a hateful look at Emily. "It wasn't his fault. The wagon wheel broke, no warning." She nodded back at the tilted wagon. People were standing around it, talking and pointing. Joey's brother Jason and his father were in between, keeping the crowd away from where Joe lay on the ground. "I saw it happen," Kiley went on. "He had his hands around her waist, but she's so light she just launched."

A horn gave a staccato series of beeps, and a Subaru rolled through the parting crowds. Doc. Sophie got out one door, black bag in hand. Her teenage son Max got out the other door and came rushing forward. Sophie went straight to Emily, her hands quickly pushing wet hair up off Tilda's face. "You okay, Tilda?"

"Daddy saved me," she said, nodding. "But he got hurted. I think his head is broken."

Sophie moved quickly to Joey, lying unconscious on the ground. She slid a neck brace beneath him and fastened it tight. Max knelt beside her, opened the medical bag and took out a soft plastic bottle of saline solution.

"Tell me everything," Sophie ordered as she squirted saline into the wound to rinse the blood away. Max aimed a penlight at the injury while she did, even though it was daylight.

"He was in the wagon, watching his daughter like a hawk," Kiley said, shooting another glare Emily's way. "The wheel broke, and he was slammed against the back. There's some metal trim along the back edge. I don't know why the hell I didn't cover it in padding. Tilda just shot up out of the wagon like she was launched from a catapult and landed in the water. Joe dove over the side and went in after her before her dress had a chance to soak through."

"So he was walking, talking?"

"Carried her right up to her mother. Then collapsed when she started screaming at him like a freaking crazy person."

The teenager shot his mom a look. Sophie was pressing clean white bandages to the back of Joey's head and wrapping it tight with gauze. Pressure, Emily figured.

Sophie said, "Okay. Kiley, Rob, you should see to your guests. Make sure no one else got hurt. Assure them Joey and

Tilda are fine." She glanced up at Tilda who was hugging her mom and crying softly.

"Is he?" Emily asked.

"I am," Joey said. It was kind of a moan, but he was trying to sit up between Sophie and Max and looking Tilda's way. "You okay, honey?"

Tilda nodded. "You bleeded a lot, Daddy. But doctor Sophie put a Band-Aid on it."

"Are you sure he doesn't need a hospital?" Emily asked Sophie. Rob was leading his hot-tempered bride Kiley away, but they stopped when they reached Bobby Joe and Jason. Some of the teenage, elf-hatted helpers gathered around Kiley and she apparently gave them instructions and sent them back to work. The crowd started to dissipate.

"You should have an X-ray," Sophie said. "Make sure you didn't crack your skull. You need a pile of stitches, too. I can do both of those things at the clinic, if you prefer it to the ER at Tucker Lake General."

He nodded. "I prefer it." Then he nodded at Emily. "Bring Tilda. She needs an exam, too."

"I'm okay, Daddy. You saved me."

Jason and his father came over, then. Jason extended a hand to his injured brother and helped him to his feet.

Sophie got up, too, kept one hand on Joey's shoulder. "Want a ride, Emily?" she asked. "You can pick up the van later. You look pretty shaken up."

She shook her head. "We'll meet you at the clinic. I need to get Tilda into dry clothes." She carried her baby to her van, cranked the motor and turned up the heat. But the whole time she kept an eye on Joey as his brother helped him into Sophie's car.

She used the blanket to rub Tilda down, looking her over head to toe while she quickly changed her clothes. You didn't have a three-year-old and not carry a spare outfit or two wherever you went. Em peeled off Tilda's pretty green dress and white tights and Dora the Explorer undies in the back of the van and checked her all over for bruises. There wasn't a single one, but she was shivering like a dry leaf in a windstorm. Quickly, Em put dry clothes on her, a pair of red and white striped leggings and a blue sweater dress with a knitted rosebud at the waist. She topped it with Tilda's spare jacket, pink with sparkles, which, she noted, was getting a little bit snug. Then she used the dry parts of the blanket to rub down her curls and buckled her into her car seat. The van was nice and warm, by then, and Tilda's shivering seemed to be slowing. Her lips were pink again, not the terrifying blue they'd been at first, and her eyes were clear.

"Hurry up, Mommy. I want to see if Daddy's okay."

"He's okay. Dr. Sophie's got him. We're going to him right now, okay?"

She nodded, then her eyes went wide. "My orange-a-mint!"

Someone tapped on the van door, and when she opened it, Emily saw Bobby Joe himself standing there, holding up a pretty little plastic, shoe-shaped ornament that was completely covered in glitter.

"I found this in the wagon," he said.

"My orange-a-mint!" Tilda took it from him and said, "Thanks, Grampa."

"You're welcome, my girl." Then he looked at Emily. "I'd like to ride to the clinic with you, if you don't mind."

Blinking, Em nodded. "All right."

He kissed Tilda's forehead, and then got into the front passenger seat. Emily double checked the car seat buckles, then closed the side door and got behind the wheel.

"I can't believe how fast he went in after her," Bobby Joe said as she pulled carefully out of the parking area, watching for children and driving slow. "Given his history with water."

Her brain had been running at full tilt until he said those

words. The myriad thoughts skidded to a stop, and she flashed back in her mind to the day Joey McIntyre had jumped from a very tall ledge into a very small koi pond, vanished beneath the water, and failed to come back up. He'd got his foot tangled in seaweed at the bottom. She was just a little girl, six years old at the time. And she'd seen the way the water churned as he struggled underneath. She'd screamed for help. His brothers had come running. They dove in and pulled him out.

She'd never seen anything so terrifying as Joey's limp body, his closed eyes, and his big brother Jason blowing air into his lungs and pumping on his chest.

He'd nearly drowned. She didn't think he'd gone swimming since. Until today.

Em quickly turned on the backseat DVD player for Tilda, so she wouldn't overhear anything she shouldn't.

"He's had a phobia ever since that day at the koi pond," Bobby Joe was saying. "That's why you could never coax him into the pool with you all those times you snuck around out there with your girlfriends."

She lifted her brows. "You knew about that?"

He nodded. "I didn't mind at all. To tell you the truth, Judith and I always hoped the two of you would end up together. Did she mention that when you saw her?"

She shook her head.

"Well, it's true. We talked about it all the time. What a perfect match you'd be for him, what beautiful babies you would make." He glanced over his seat at Tilda, and his face went sappy sweet. "We were right."

She turned a corner. The clinic was only a couple of miles away, but maybe it was time for her to take this particular bull by the horns. "I'd like to hear your side of it," she said. "This thing that happened between you and my father. I'd like to know what he said to you, what you said to him."

He sighed deeply, glanced into the back to be sure Tilda

wasn't listening. A glance in the mirror told Em she was completely involved in the DVD she was watching.

"I won't speak ill of the dead," Bobby Joe said at length. "Your father's actions that day were completely out of character, and in hindsight, I wish I hadn't fired him for it. He panicked, and he was doing what he thought was best for you. As a father myself, I can't hold that against him."

"He told you I was pregnant," she said. "And that Joey was the father."

Bobby Joe nodded. "And that you'd already made your decision. Were already in the process of carrying it out. He talked about you being the first member of his family to go to college, and your future, and your genius, and how the family name was on your shoulders." He lowered his head. "I couldn't tell Joey. It would've broken his heart. I should have known better. I knew you, had watched you grow up. I should've known. But I took Henry's word for it."

She nodded. "And the money?"

"He asked for it. I might have offered anyway, if he hadn't. I don't know. But not to bribe you or influence you. If it were left to me, I'd have tried to bribe you to keep her. Not the opposite." Then he shrugged. "I don't have any proof of that. I realize you have to choose to believe me or believe your own father, and I don't blame you if you choose him."

She nodded.

"I don't blame him for trying to look out for you, Emily," he said. "You were everything to him. He hung every hope he ever had on you. Judith used to say it was too heavy a load to put on one little girl's shoulders. She always worried he expected too much from you. That you'd never feel you had lived up to his hopes and dreams for you, no matter how well you might do in life."

She blinked and glanced sideways at him. "That's exactly

how I've felt since…since I can remember. That my father's happiness was all up to me."

"To Henry, the pregnancy threatened everything he had planned for you, every hope he had for your future."

She nodded. "I believe that, too."

Bobby Joe nodded. "Whatever you choose to believe about me, and what happened that day, Emily, I want to be very clear on this. Joey never knew. Not any of it. And that little girl back there means more to me than I can even tell you. I'd cut out my own heart out to make her well. That's the truth. Everything I've told you is the truth."

She looked over at him and was surprised to see tears pooling in his eyes. And then she was pulling into the driveway of the big old Victorian that housed the Big Falls Family Clinic.

CHAPTER ELEVEN

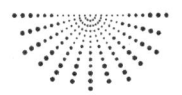

Two hours and thirteen stitches later, Joey was propped up in his own bed, in his room above the Long Branch, staring at the door and making escape plans. His brothers were downstairs, and so were his father and Vidalia. Bobby Joe was greeting the patrons personally tonight. Kiley, Rob and Jason were doing everything else. And Vidalia was, as far as he could tell, on guard dog duty. If he so much as put a toe out of bed, she was chasing him right back into it again. There was no escape.

And then there was a soft knock at the door. It couldn't be Vidalia. She hadn't knocked once.

"Come on in," he called.

At first it was no one. The door opened, and there was only a view of the hallway beyond it. Then he sat up on his elbows and saw them. Tilda had a little wooden tray in her two hands. It had to be heavy, with its plate of goodies and steaming mugs and the little rosebud in a blue glass bud vase. He could see her innocent smile behind the rosebud, her dimples...even in her chin. The way her eyes smiled as much as her lips. And right behind her, crouching low, her hands over Tilda's on the tray,

Emily. Her eyes were on his, uncertain and worried. And maybe a little bit sorry. Her strawberry and honey hair cascaded right down to Tilda's, whose head just reached Emily's chin. You couldn't tell whose curls were whose beyond that point.

Emily shuffled the two of them into the room, somehow maintaining her crouch, all the way up to the side of his bed. She helped Tilda lift the tray toward him, and he took it and settled it on his lap. "This looks amazing. Thank you," he said to Tilda. He didn't care what the tray held. He was just glad to see her looking so good. So normal. Like nothing had happened.

Tilda smiled and held out her arms. He reached for her, but Emily scooped her up first. "Ah-ah. Concussion protocol, Joey."

"Concussion protocol?"

"Tell him, Tilda." Emily set Tilda on the mattress next to him.

She counted off on her stubby little fingers. "Stay in bed. Take it *easy*. No excursion."

Exertion, Em mouthed.

He sat up a little higher and put his arm around Tilda's shoulders

"Mommy said you needed us," she told him seriously.

"I've needed you for a long time now, sweet thing."

She smiled and hugged his neck.

"Caref—" Em began, but he held up a hand before she finished.

"It's good, all good." Tilda felt so tiny, so fragile in his arms. His heart filled with pure love. He couldn't lose this little girl. The full force of that possibility had hit him like never before in those terrifying moments she'd spent in the water. The magnitude of it, the devastation. It just couldn't happen. He wouldn't survive it, and neither would Emily.

Tilda finished hugging him and sat back down beside him, simultaneously taking a brownie from the tray he hadn't even looked at yet.

"Tilda, those are for your dad."

"Daddies always share, Mom." Leaning back on her pillow, she took a bite and chewed. Chocolate lined her lips. He felt himself tearing up.

Emily was looking at him, he realized, and he blinked his eyes dry and tried to distract himself by checking out the tray's contents. The platter of cookies and brownies didn't even tempt him, but the coffee, that looked like heaven. He reached for the mug and took a big sip of its dark, bitter goodness. "Oh, that's fantastic. Thank you."

Only then did he dare look Em's way. She wasn't fooled. Her eyes were searching, probing, maybe understanding what he was feeling. That must be what she'd been feeling in those moments when she'd arrived to see her baby being carried soaking wet from a raging river.

A tap on the door drew his gaze. Vidalia stood there, leaning in. "You all doing okay? Need anything?"

Emily looked her way and nodded. Then glanced pointedly at Tilda, lying curled up beside him.

"I sure could use some help downstairs," Vidalia said, translating the message perfectly. "You wouldn't want to give me a hand, would you Matilda?"

"Can I?" she asked.

"You sure can. I'll bring you back up here to your dad in a few minutes, okay?" Vidalia held out her arms.

Tilda looked at her mom. Emily nodded, and then Joey got a peck on the cheek. "See you later, elevator!" She slid off the bed and shot out the door. Vidalia pulled it closed as she ran off after her.

"Think Vidalia can keep up?" he asked.

Emily had been looking at the closed door, but she turned to face him then. Before she could say anything, he said, "Sophie check her over?"

"Yeah. She's fine. No harm done. Not even a bruise."

"Thank God."

"Thank *you*." She moved closer to the bed. "I shouldn't have yelled at you like I did. I was near hysterics, seeing her like that. I didn't know or care what I was saying. It was wrong and I'm sorry, and I know it wasn't your fault, and I am so *damn* grateful to you for saving her life..." She stopped talking, but he didn't think it was by choice. More like her words got choked off.

"I'm sorry I let that happen."

"It wasn't your fault, Joey. I couldn't have done any better if I'd been the one in the wagon with her. And you went into the water after her. And you haven't gone into the water since you nearly drowned in the koi pond."

"I couldn't think of anything but getting to her."

She lowered her head. "You're a true father. You really are."

He couldn't talk. Couldn't respond. His voice just left him, along with all his breath. He didn't think a higher compliment existed.

Then she looked up. "Now, tell me what's wrong. I can see there's something."

He pressed his lips, patted the side of the bed. "Sit down. Have a brownie with me. Drink some of my coffee."

"There's a whole pot downstairs." But she sat down, took a chocolate chip cookie and a big sip of his coffee, then grimaced because it was black and bitter.

"You ever wonder what would have happened if you'd just told me?" he asked.

"It haunts me. I've been wondering that ever since I found out you didn't really know. I've wondered it about a million times. I wake up at night wondering about it."

He nodded slow. "I'd have asked you to marry me. That would've been my first instinct. Dad told us three our whole lives, from age eleven or so, when we thought he was being gross, 'you make a girl pregnant, you marry her.' I grew up with that drilled into my brain."

She nodded. "I was so in love, I'd have said yes."

"I'd have taken care of her while you finished school," he said.

"But then your dad would've got sick and you'd have had to leave."

"I'd have brought you with me."

"I couldn't have left. Not and had my career, my business."

"We'd have found a way." He took the tray off his lap and set it on the night stand.

She breathed slowly, deeply. "We were so young. Do you think we could've made it work? You and me? Together?"

"I don't know. You're right, we were younger. I was stupider. I really don't know."

"Maybe we'd have screwed it up," she said. "Maybe it was too soon for us."

"Maybe it's not too soon anymore." He slid his hands around hers, fisted there in her lap. "Maybe this could be a new start for us. Maybe *this* is the right time."

She lifted her head, met his eyes and stared into them. "I still feel everything I did before," she whispered. "Only…there's so much more depth to be explored. It's like looking into deep, dark water, getting ready to dive in. You just don't know what you're gonna find."

"Respectfully, hon, you're a whole lot darker and deeper than I am." He opened his arms, palms up. "What you see is what you get. I don't know how to not wear everything on my sleeve. I don't know how to hide my feelings. My water is crystal clear. No hidden rocks or seaweed waiting to tangle you up on the bottom. I promise."

She took a breath. "I'm full of jagged-edged rocks and probably even a few sharks." Then her eyes plumbed his, and she said, "You'd be crazy to jump in."

"I already jumped. I'm in the water. So…contain your sharks, woman." He leaned forward, cupped her head, pulled her closer and kissed her long and slow and deep. His heart beat faster and he wrapped his arms more completely around her, pulling her closer.

"No strenuous activity for seventy-two hours," she whispered against his mouth. "And absolutely no excursion."

He smiled, but didn't move his lips away from hers. He kissed her again, and again. Until she slid lower on the bed, out of his arms, out of his reach. Sighing, he lay back again and took a brownie from the bedside stand. "You restored my appetite."

"Tell me what you and Doc Sophie were talking about when Tilda and I got there," she said. "I could see it wasn't good. And if those tears in your eyes when you were holding her earlier were from the same cause, then...."

He didn't answer for a long moment, but then he decided he had to.

"Sophie has most of the test results back," he said, and he could see her bracing. "So far, no one's a match."

Her spine went stiffer. He could see her steeling herself, trying to be strong. "Most of the results? Who's still out?"

"Mine, Dad's, and Jason's.

She lowered her head. "Selene didn't match then?"

"No."

"That means your father won't either. She was his donor, you said."

He nodded.

"So we're down to two chances," she said.

He shook his head. "Plus twenty-six," he said. "Vidalia's family in Texas is getting tested. A bunch of them are coming up for Christmas."

She frowned. "Because of Tilda?"

He shrugged. "She's the newest member of their family. And she's in trouble. Their family motto is 'when one Brand is in trouble, every Brand is in trouble.' And to them, she's a Brand."

She stared into his eyes. "She's a McIntyre."

"That's true. And that means she'll be fine. One McIntyre already beat this thing. A precedent's been set."

"Blood relatives are her best chance, Joey."

"But not her only chance," he said. "You hang in there. She's not sick yet."

She nodded, slid higher up on the bed, snuggled into the circle of his arm. It felt good holding her there, right up until he started looking around the room and seeing it through her eyes.

"I was going to gut the whole second story, turn it into a giant bachelor pad."

"I can imagine."

He nodded. "But now I've decided to leave it as is."

"You gonna keep living in a glorified hotel room?"

He shook his head. "I'm gonna build a house." He nodded toward the rear-facing window. "Out that way. There's twenty acres. Plenty of room. I'll make a fenced-in back yard and get a big slobbery dog."

She smiled, staring out the window, envisioning it, he thought. "That's nice."

"It will be." He rolled onto his side, so he could stare down into her eyes. "Move in here," he said. "We have an empty room."

"You want to move Tilda from a beautiful Inn with no other guests and a backyard playground to a room above a bar?"

"It's not that kind of a bar."

"It's still a bar. No playground. No privacy. No room." She made a face. "I think you see my dilemma here."

"I do."

She heaved a sigh and said, "Besides, I don't want to move too fast, Joe. I don't want to get her hopes up only to have things not work out."

He could see plainly in her eyes that she wasn't just talking about Tilda there. "Okay," he said. "Okay. So...you wanna go into Tucker Lake with me tomorrow? We'll do some Christmas shopping, maybe go out to lunch, make a day of it."

"I don't know, Joey. That sounds a lot like an excursion."

He grinned and kissed her again.

Emily slid to her feet when they heard footsteps in the hall. She smoothed her clothes and faced the door as it opened. Tilda walked in, clutching Vidalia's hand. "Well now, it's all worked out! Isn't it?"

"Shoooore is," Tilda sang.

"What's all worked out?" Joey asked. He reached out and clasped Emily's hand, gave it a warning squeeze. Vidalia's eyes had that certain sparkle in them that they got sometimes.

"The Texans are comin'," Vidalia explained.

"The Texans are comin', the Texans are comin'!" Tilda danced around the room. "We have more aunties and uncles and cousins, Mommy! Lots of them, and they're all comin' for Christmas!"

"That's right," Vidalia said. "Joey, we're going to need every room in the Long Branch and at Ida Mae's, and every spare bedroom the rest of us can vacate. Dax is already packing up. He's gonna bunk in with Jason, since he's a bachelor, out at that falling-down smithy shop of his. And the three of you are going to stay in the old hunting cabin, up near the falls."

"The *three* of us?" Emily parroted.

"What old hunting cabin?" Joey asked. "I never heard of any old hunting cabin."

"Belonged to my first husband," Vidalia said. "Been on the market for years. Betty Lou's been keeping it up for us. You've met Betty Lou, Emily."

"I treated her dog."

"She's our town realtor. Great lady. Anyway, that cabin is perfectly usable, just so far off the beaten path it doesn't appeal to most buyers. Well, Betty Lou's getting it ready for you tonight. And the girls and I will do our thing, you know."

Emily sent Joey a look that plainly asked what *their thing* was.

"It's the *perfect* spot," Tilda said dramatically. "We'll have our own tree!"

"It's only for the next few days. Oh, and it's a really cozy place. You'll love it!"

"And Grammy V's gonna tell Santa, so he can find us." Tilda put a hand beside her mouth and stage whispered, "She *knows* him."

"We'll move you in tomorrow," Vidalia said, then sent an apologetic look at Emily. "I know this is a terrible inconvenience, dear. And of course you can say no if you want to, I just..." she shrugged. "I don't know, call me old fashioned, but I just feel Tilda will be so much happier in a real home with her own tree and decorations for Christmas. Don't you?"

"I..." she looked at Joey, then at Tilda.

"Please, Mommy?"

Vidalia watched her with raised eyebrows, then said, "Emily?" and inclined her head toward the hallway.

She wanted a private word, so Emily ducked out into the hallway, and Vidalia closed the door. Joey wondered what was being said out there. Emily hadn't had a mother figure, ever, that he knew of. And Vidalia tended to want to be everyone's. Even poor pathetic, heartbroken Dax down the hall.

The door opened, and Emily came back in alone. She met his eyes. He said, "Well?"

She sighed. "Well, we're moving into a hunting cabin tomorrow."

"Yay!" Tilda was smiling ear to ear. "Just like a real family!"

~

Emily and Tilda packed up all their stuff—and it was a lot of stuff—and hauled their bags down the stairs to the van, one by one. Ida Mae was wringing her hands and looking worried the whole time. She stood on the front porch, gingham dress, white apron, silver gray hair like a cap made of curls. She was the epitome of a small-town innkeeper.

"I'm real sorry you're being put out like this," she said, following them outside, but remaining on the porch as they loaded the van. "I just don't understand why Vidalia would ask it of you. Those Texas Brands could just as easily bunk in the hunting cabin themselves."

"That's what I thought, too," Emily said. "But then I had a private talk with her. The truth is, she's worried about Joey. That was a pretty serious blow to the head he took. She wants to make sure someone's close by to keep an eye on him."

"Joey?" Ida Mae's worried look vanished. One eyebrow rose and she crossed her arms over her chest. "Joey's staying at the cabin with you?"

"That's the plan."

The older woman's face broke into a delighted smile, all hint of worry gone. "That's nice. I mean, it'll be nice for Tilda." And then she sent a quick glance at Tilda and a hint of her former worry returned to her eyes. "She's doing all right?"

Joey had been right when he'd said that everyone in town knew about Tilda's condition, her prognosis and the search for donors. And before too long, they'd probably all know about Emily's new living arrangements, as well. Nobody in Big Falls seemed too concerned about privacy. And yet it wasn't a busybody kind of place. It was more…it was more like they just all cared. A lot.

"I'll miss you, young lady," Ida Mae said. "You'd better come by for tea and cookies in the sun room every now and then."

Tilda smiled brightly. "I promise!" Then she ran back up the porch steps and gave Ida Mae a big hug. Em thought Ida Mae got a little misty before Tilda raced back to the van, jumped in, and got into her car seat without any help at all.

Emily walked up the porch steps and Ida Mae hugged her, too. "Joey's a good man," she said to Emily.

"I know that, Ida Mae."

Then she sniffled and said, "You should bring her to church soon, so everyone who's been praying for her has the chance to meet her."

She blinked. "They've been praying for her?"

"Ever since you got here. Vidalia's prayer group has met at the church every night this week to petition our Lord on behalf of that little angel." She shrugged. "We do that from time to time when we need big help."

Emily blinked, her eyes getting hot. "Does it work?"

"You'd be surprised how often it does. You keep your chin up, Emily. You've gotta have faith."

She didn't have. She hadn't had faith in much of anything since Tilda's diagnosis. But coming here…her faith in Joey had been restored, her faith in his father was beginning to heal. Her faith in family, in friends…that was coming together too. She was even beginning to find a level of acceptance for what her father had done, if not quite forgiveness. She was closer. "Thank you," she said softly.

"Thank *you*. For bringing Tilda here to us. And for helping Betty Lou with her dog. She's part of the prayer group too, you know. Oh, and Rollo is feeling much better today, thanks to you."

"I'm glad I had antibiotics on hand for him. Tell her Rollo needs to stay away from road kill from now on."

She went back to the van, got in and pulled away. Ida Mae waved until they were out of sight, and Emily sighed. She was starting to love this town. These people. She was starting to feel as if this might be the right place to raise her little girl, if she was lucky enough to have that chance.

Following Vidalia's directions, Emily turned off Main Street and drove up, up, up, over winding dirt roads without any road signs, that twisted through the hilliest part of the state. She couldn't stop imagining Vidalia and her friends, women like Ida

Mae and Betty Lou, mature women, wise women, the matriarchs of Big Falls, led by their pastor, gathering at that beautiful country church to pray for Tilda. It was a wonderful image, and it felt warm in her chest.

It wasn't hard to spot the cabin. There were two mini-vans and two pickup trucks, one of them Joey's, parked wherever there was room. They'd left her a spot in the driveway, which she appreciated.

It was a log cabin, one story, with big windows. The logs had aged to a dark, rich brown, and the stuff in between the logs was bleached white, creating a contrasting look that was somehow beautiful. A big cobblestone chimney rose up on one side. Add a little snow and put a wreath on the door, and it could be a Currier and Ives Christmas card.

It did not look much like an old hunting cabin that had been standing empty for years.

As Emily got out of the van, several of Vidalia's daughters came out the front door, laughing and chattering, all wearing sweaters and hats in deference to the chill of the morning. They spotted her and looked even more cheerful, if that was possible, and they all headed for the van.

"Oh thank goodness you're here!" Maya said. "You might have better luck making Joey stay still than we've had."

"His brothers just went out for a load of firewood, and the minute they left, he started trying to work!" Kara added.

"Doesn't know the meaning of 'no strenuous activity,'" Mel said.

"He did seem to understand when you said stay down or you'd knock him down, though," Edie put in.

Mel shrugged and laughed. Angel-haired Selene remained quiet, reaching out to help Tilda unbuckle, then scooping her up. "I have an early present for you, Miss Tilda Louise."

"A present?"

"Um-hm." She handed her a little box with a ribbon on top.

Emily watched as Tilda opened the box. Her eyes rounded as she pulled on a green ribbon out of the box, and saw a large crystal prism dangling from the end. "It's a *treasure!*"

Selene smiled. "If you hang it in your bedroom window, it will make rainbows on your walls whenever the sunshine hits it. And I put some magic in it, too."

"You did?" Tilda asked, looking up wide eyed.

"Mm-hm. Guaranteed to keep away nightmares and anything nasty."

"Wow. Thank you...."

"Aunt Selene," Selene filled in.

Tilda's smile was huge, and she draped the ribbon around her neck. Not exactly its intended use, but still.

"What a beautiful gift," Emily said. "Thank you, Selene."

"You bet." She took Tilda's hand. "Let's go inside and show your dad." She glanced Emily's way. "That okay?"

"Sure." They really had taken to Tilda, this family.

As soon as Tilda was out of earshot, Maya put a hand on Emily's arm, and said, "We're really sorry Mom did this to you."

"She's so transparent it's not even funny," Mel said. "Sticking the three of you out here together."

"She should teach a class." Edie glanced toward the cabin with an eye roll. "Vidalia Brand McIntyre's Meddling 101."

"So...you're saying she's trying to...."

"She thinks you'll fall madly in love if you just spend some time alone together," Kara said, hauling a couple of suitcases out of the back of the van.

"Selene's no help," Maya put in. "Keeps saying it's fate." She glanced at Emily. "She's a Wiccan, you know."

"Joey mentioned it."

"You can change your mind about staying here and head right back to Ida Mae's. No one would blame you," Edie told her.

They all seemed to go silent then, looking at her, waiting.

She shrugged. "I think Tilda is going to love being with both of her parents for Christmas. I just…I don't want her to get her hopes up that this will be… you know…"

"Permanent," Edie said, sighing.

Maya nodded. "I tried to tell Mom that. None of us want Tilda to be hurt. None of us."

"She's why the entire Texas branch of the family is coming up for Christmas, you know," Kara said. "It's all about your little girl. They want to help."

"That's…kind of amazing." Emily's voice had gone whispery.

"It's what our family's about. Always has been," Mel said.

"Tilda's impossible not to love. Mom sent pics, told them about her…condition." Maya was smiling, despite the topic. "They called a family meeting, dropped all their holiday plans and started packing."

"You have to love our family," Kara said, grabbing the last bag from the back of the van, then heading into the cabin.

"Yeah," Emily whispered, watching her go. "Yeah, you kind of do."

∼

Joey had arrived to a damp, chilly, empty cabin with a slightly musty aroma to it. But four hours later, it had been completely transformed. The main section of the place was an open floor plan with the kitchen on one side, taking up a little less than half the space, and a living room on the other side, taking up the rest. A countertop island marked the border between the two. There were two bedrooms, kitty-corner from each other with a bathroom in between.

By the time the women of his family had finished "doing their thing," the place had been transformed into a cozy country cabin with checkered curtains in the kitchen windows and frilly green ones everywhere else. A love seat, rocking chair, and coffee table were positioned on a big throw rug in the living room, facing a TV set. No cable or dish, but there was a DVD player and a stack of holiday movies donated by Maya. The beds were old, but the mattresses, pillows and bedding were brand new. His father had money and he wasn't shy about spending it. The kitchen was fully stocked. The old fridge had been cleaned until it sparkled, and then filled with groceries. Ditto the cupboards. There was at least a face cord of firewood stacked outside, just to the left of the front door, and a huge supply of it had been carried in to fill the log holder beside the fireplace, which was snapping and crackling like crazy.

At long last, everyone had left. There was a casserole warming in the oven, alongside cinnamon rolls that filled the place with their delicious aroma. A pot full of coffee was calling his name.

Emily sat on the love seat, Tilda snuggled up in her lap. Joey was tending to dinner because no one had let him do much of anything else all day, and he was done with that. Emily had worked like a trooper and was probably exhausted. Her head was tilted to one side, her eyes closed. Tilda's head rested on her shoulder, and her eyes were closed, too.

Silently, he tugged his phone out of his pocket, lifted it, and took a picture of them. A pair of exhausted angels, getting some well-deserved rest after a busy day.

The shutter click sound effect served no other purpose than to wake them up. He pocketed the phone and said, "Dinner is served."

"Smells delicious. But you should've let me," Emily said.

"It wasn't the least bit strenuous. And thanks to my family, it was the first productive thing I've been allowed to do today. My ego needed it."

She smiled. "They're something, your family."

"Hate to break it to you, Em, but they're your family, too. As Tilda's mommy, you're in."

She grinned. "That's gonna take some getting used to for an only child with no family at all."

"You um..." He lowered his eyes, straightened some silverware on the table that wasn't crooked. "You planning to stick around long enough to do that? Get used to it?"

She held his eyes for a second, then looked away. "Tilda, you want to eat some dinner?"

"I wanna get a Christmas tree."

"It's been a long day, honey. Maybe we can get the tree tomorrow."

Her face twisted up the way it did when she was about to start crying. Her bottom lip thrust out, and her eyes teared up. "But I want a Christmas tree!"

"Okay, okay, cool, we've got this," Joey said quickly. "Let's eat dinner, and then we'll get a tree. All right? The place in town is open for another..." he looked at his phone, and saw the picture he'd snapped of the two of them. His heart turned to mush.

"You can't say yes to everything she asks for Joey," Emily said. "Just because she cries...."

"Aw, come on," he said. "I want a Christmas tree, too." He pointed to the big picture window along the front of the living room. "I had them leave that spot empty just so we could fit our tree there. And Gramma V left us a tree stand and a box full of decorations. What do you think, Tilda? Good spot?"

"Perfect," Tilda replied.

Emily looked from one of them to the other, then shrugged and said, "I'm not gonna stand a chance against the two of you, am I?"

Joey looked at Tilda and winked. Tilda's giggle was as evil as a three-year-old angel could manage.

CHAPTER TWELVE

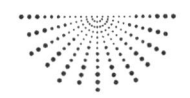

They chose a tree from the pre-cut ones at the lot in the village. It was across from the big circular park that split Main Street like a boulder splits a river. Many of Big Falls' most popular businesses were situated on one side of that split or the other, and every year, a local tree farmer set up his Christmas tree stand in the same spot.

Joey would've preferred to take Tilda out to a cut-your-own place, but Emily said this was better. Faster, easier, and less... strenuous. If he heard that word one more time....

Still, Tilda picked the fattest evergreen on the lot, and the proprietor had his son load it for them, because everyone in town knew Joey was supposed to be taking it easy.

An hour later, they were back at the cabin.

"It's beautiful," Tilda said, standing back and admiring it. Then she gasped and raced into the bedroom where all her stuff had been unpacked, and came back with the shoe ornament she'd made out at Holiday Ranch. Carefully, reverently, she placed it on a branch.

Joey got tears in his eyes. "That's perfect, sweetie," he said.

"We need lights." Tilda said. But she smiled at her treasure, pushing it so it swung back and forth on its branch, and then she yawned.

"I think there are some in the box of decorations from Grandma V," Emily said.

"And if there aren't enough," Joey added, "then we'll go Christmas shopping tomorrow and get as many lights as you want."

"Okay." Then she turned to him and held up her arms. "It's bedtime now. Will you tell me a story?"

He picked her up. "You bet I will. But first, you've gotta put on your jammies and brush those pearly whites." He sent Emily a look, and she nodded her approval. Yes, he was getting this right. And it looked like she was going to let him have this bedtime routine all to himself.

"Okay, Daddy," Tilda said, and he carried her into the bedroom where Emily had put her things.

While he was tucking her in, Emily came in for a few minutes to say goodnight to Tilda. She gave her a big loving hug and kissed her all over her beautiful little face, and then she left them alone again. She was willingly giving him some space to be a daddy, and he was grateful.

There were approximately a dozen story books to choose from. Tilda said she had lots more at home, but had brought only her very favorites.

He read Dr. Seuss's *Terrible Tongue Twisters* to her, and she laughed at him every time he messed up. They tried to say the silly rhymes together, and after a while, her eyes started falling closed despite her best efforts to keep them open.

He read a little more, but slower, softer, pausing in between pages for long deep breaths. And within a few minutes, Tilda was sound asleep.

Joey closed the book and set it on the rustic nightstand that was made from birch logs, just like the beds and dressers in both bedrooms. And then he sat there looking at her for a long moment as she lay sound asleep on the bed.

It was kind of amazing, how thoroughly his life had changed in just a matter of days. He was in love again. He was only just realizing he'd never quite fallen out of love with Emily. And now that love was multiplied by infinity, because Tilda was a part of it too.

He'd talked to his cousin Sophie at length while she'd been stitching up his head at the clinic. She said she should have the rest of the test results within another day or two, but she hadn't sounded all that optimistic about finding a match. All of the Texas Brands would be getting tested, too. Sophie was opening the clinic to make room for them all to come in for blood draws, despite it being a holiday weekend.

Day after tomorrow was Christmas Eve, he realized. And with all that had happened, he hadn't yet finished his shopping. He needed a gift for Emily. He had something in mind, but he'd have to get it from his mother in Texas before the big day. He'd purchased approximately a pickup truckload of presents for Tilda, including the most realistic baby doll to be found, and a firetruck pedal car. Wade Armstrong, Edie's husband, had that at his shop and was installing a siren. Realistic but quieter, he'd said.

Joe tucked the covers carefully around his little girl and then rose and walked softly out of the bedroom. Emily was by the fireplace, adding another log. She dropped it carefully, and a shower of sparks hissed and flew up the chimney. Then she replaced the screen and stood there staring at the flames, her back to him, strawberry blond curls hanging down her clingy green sweater.

"This was a good idea," he said.

She looked back at him. "You think?"

"I do." He pulled the bedroom door partly closed.

"I do, too. I think it's good...for Tilda."

He nodded. "And maybe for us, too."

She closed her eyes. "Frankly, I've been sitting here trying to figure out why you don't hate me after all I've done to you."

"I could never hate you. I've been angry, yeah. But I've never hated you, Emily. I've pretty much been stupid in love with you since the day we first met."

"We were barely out of diapers the day we first met," she said.

"And it was over for me." He pressed a hand to his chest, where his heart was pounding pretty solidly. "I've been bleeding since you left me, Em. And that's nothing but the truth." He moved up behind her, slid a hand over her shoulder.

She tipped her head sideways, brushed her cheek across his hand. "We haven't even been in the same state for years, Joey. We're different people—"

"I know that. And I know there's no guarantee we're still..."

"Compatible?" She tipped her head back against his chest.

"I don't even know what that means. I don't think it's even a real thing. We're humans, not machines. We're...pliable."

"Mutable." She turned then, looked up at him. "We can choose to make it work, is that what you mean?"

"That's what my sister Selene would say. Did say, matter of fact."

"You...discussed me with her?"

He nodded. "She knows things. I can't explain it."

"And what does she know about us?" she asked. She was looking up at him with those big blue eyes wide open and sparkling like ocean water over a white sand bottom.

"She says it's destiny. She says we came together so early in life because we just plain couldn't wait. That we're soulmates. And that there's no use fighting it."

Emily blinked rapidly.

"She and her um...group...did a healing ritual for Tilda the other night. She asked permission and I gave it. I hope that's okay with you."

She nodded. "Vidalia's prayer group has been doing something similar. I haven't believed in anything for a long time, but I guess it's good to cover all the bases." A little smile, a little hope in her eyes.

"We should be together, Emily. We should choose to make it work for our daughter." For whatever time we have with her, he thought, but he didn't say it out loud. He didn't have to.

She looked at his lips, and then into his eyes. "You're still the best kisser in existence," she whispered.

He was smiling when he kissed her, wrapped his arms around her waist and pulled her up onto her toes against his chest. She nibbled on his lower lip, and he stumbled them toward the second bedroom and through its door. They fell onto the bed together, a tangle of limbs and lips and hands eagerly trying to remove clothing. Their own, each other's. And somehow in the chaos, they wound up naked, and she was pressed against him, every inch of them touching. His chest pressed against her breasts, and her hands ran up and down his back. His hairy calves moved slow against her smooth ones, and she shivered when he caressed her neck with his bristly cheek. She threw a pillow at the door to push it closed without even breaking their kiss.

He paused for a second, right there, and lifted his head a little so he could look at her. And he thought what a gift it was that she'd come back to him and about how he'd never felt for any other girl the way he'd felt for Emily. Not from day one, and not even since she'd run away.

She bit his lip a little harder than before to get his attention, and then smiling, she clutched his hips, and pulled him to her.

And Joey McIntyre's thoughts came to a grinding halt, because he went to heaven for a little while.

∼

Emily was asleep, all wrapped up in Joey's arms, her head on his chest, when she heard Tilda coughing.

She came awake immediately, as only moms can do, and was on her feet and dressed in about three seconds.

The bed rustled as she opened the door, and Joey muttered "Whuz-wrong?"

"She's coughing." Emily hurried past the Christmas tree, and noticed the whole house smelled of pine as she headed into Tilda's room. She had kicked off all her covers and was curled up and hugging herself as if she were freezing. "Okay Tilda baby, it's okay. Mamma's here." Emily got onto the bed and gathered her close, holding her, touching her face. "She's burning up," she said, looking back.

Joey was in the doorway pulling a shirt on. He already had his cellphone in his hand. "I'm calling Sophie."

Emily met his eyes and saw a mirror of everything she was feeling. Dread. Horror. Fear.

"Come on, baby, come on." Emily gathered Tilda up and carried her into the bathroom.

Joey was right behind her. "Sophie? Yeah, sorry to wake you. Tilda's coughing and has a high fever.

"Turn on the tub, Joey. Make the water cool," Emily said.

He leaned over, depressed the stopper, cranked the taps, and held one hand under the flow. "Sophie just said the same thing." He pulled the phone away from his ear and hit the speaker button. Then he set it on the edge of the sink and returned to the tub. "How cool?"

"Not too cold," Sophie said through the phone. "We don't want to shock her, just bring her temperature down. The water should be cool to the touch, but not cold. Comfortable swimming temperature."

Emily knelt beside the tub and bent over it to lower Tilda gently into the deepening, cool water.

"Is it too cold?" Joey asked.

"No. It's just right, I think." Em met his eyes. "I'm glad you're here."

"I'm glad I'm here, too," he told her. He bent over the tub beside her, and started scooping water up over the parts of Tilda that weren't immersed. He carefully wet down her hair until all the little curls hung more or less straight against her pale skin.

"I'm cold, Mommy," she murmured.

"I know, baby, I know."

Sophie said, "Can you get some ibuprofen down her, Em?"

"Yeah. I know the dose."

"I'll get it," Joe offered.

"The little blue makeup bag, Joe. It's somewhere in our… um…in the other bedroom."

He ran to get the medication and returned with both the liquid and the chewables. "Which one?"

Emily looked at Tilda. Fresh tears spilled. God this couldn't be it. This couldn't be the deadly disease waking up, ready to take her little girl away. It couldn't be. "She's barely awake," she whispered.

"Em?" Joey prompted. He put a hand on her shoulder, and it infused her with something. Strength. "The liquid. A full dropper," she said.

He nodded, opened the bottle, filled the dropper to its top mark, and handed it over. Then he got his arms around Tilda to hold her up, so Emily could try to get the meds into her.

She managed it lovingly, whispering, "Just swallow, baby. It'll make you feel better. That's my girl. That's my precious girl."

Tilda swallowed the stuff and made a face.

"We need to get her to the ER, Emily," Sophie said from the phone. "I'll come over with the EMTs so I can ride in the ambulance with her. That means you'll have to follow, but she's safer if I ride with her. Okay?"

"Okay." The word was robotic, automatic. Em's eyes had gone kind of hollow.

"You sit tight. Keep her cool. You can take her out of the tub if she starts to cool down, but put her right back in if that fever creeps up again. I'll be there in fifteen minutes. Okay?"

"Okay."

Joey hung up the phone, then stared at it for a long time. Then he lifted his gaze and looked at Emily. "We need to text our family, Em."

Blinking back tears, Emily nodded.

~

It was, Emily thought, the longest ride of her life. Tilda and Sophie and some EMTs she didn't know were just ahead in the ambulance. Tilda was so sick she couldn't even stay awake for more than a few seconds at a time.

Joey drove. She didn't know how he managed it, because he was as terrified as she was.

"Maybe it was the tree," Emily said. "Maybe she's allergic to pine. Lots of people are."

He nodded hard. "Kids get sick," he said. "We don't know for sure it's the Sanguine Morbo becoming active."

"It could be a cold. The flu," Emily said.

"It could be a pine allergy. Like you said. That makes sense. I shouldn't have given in and got the tree."

"Pine trees never bothered her before, though." She looked at him. The dashboard lights glowed on his face. He looked as frightened as she felt. "You had to get the tree. It's almost Christmas." Then she closed her eyes. "It's almost

Christmas." And then she just lowered her head into her hands and wept.

Joey reached across the space between them, pulled her closer, and she buried her head on his shoulder. "I'm sorry, I'm sorry, I'm sorry," she whispered. "I'm so, so sorry."

"It's all right, Em."

"I kept her from you. And I was wrong. I was so wrong."

"It doesn't matter now."

"What if she doesn't make it, Joe? What if it *is* the disease? Once the symptoms hit, it's fast. Days, Sophie said."

He squeezed her tighter. "We can't think that way."

"I can't do it. I can't live if she doesn't."

He squeezed her harder. "Don't give up on her yet, Emily."

Then the ambulance turned, driving right up to the ER doors, and he steered the pickup to the nearest parking spot. Em was jumping out almost before he shut off the engine, and together they ran into the hospital.

~

"Is it…the SM?" Joey asked two hours later when Sophie finally emerged from the treatment room and joined the family to give them some answers. She stood in the hallway, because the ER waiting room was full to capacity with Joey's brothers, his father, Vidalia and her daughters, their husbands, their kids. There were more Brands coming and going in groups. Emily had been introduced to more handsome, rugged Texans in the past hour than she'd thought existed, and their wives.

Everyone in the room seemed to hold their breath waiting for Sophie's answer. And when it came, it didn't help much.

"We don't know what it is yet," she said. "We have to wait for labs to come back. It'll be morning before we can tell you anything for sure. What we do know is that she's a very sick little girl. At the very least, she has pneumonia. But her fever is down now and we have her on IV antibiotics." She opened her mouth again, then closed it, lowered her head, shook it slowly.

"What?" Emily asked. "What is it?"

Sophie sighed but met her eyes. They were wet, and that scared the hell out of her. "The blood tests we ran on the family came back. All of them. No one's a match. I'm sorry."

It hit her like a tidal wave, just sort of knocked her backwards. She crashed into Joey, and his arms snapped tight around her.

"Run them again. Run mine again," Joey said. "I'm the best chance. Run mine again. Just in case."

"I will. And don't give up hope, Joe. We have thirty-six new samples to test as of today from Vidalia's Texans."

"I need to go to her," Emily said. "She's probably scared."

"She's charming the socks off the nurses. Go ahead, go on back. Just two at a time, though. We have to admit her. We'll be moving her up to Peds as soon as there's a room ready."

Emily felt another chunk of her heart crack and fall to the ground. "Tomorrow's Christmas Eve," she whispered. I don't want her to spend Christmas in the hospital."

"I know," Joey said, hugging her closer. "I know."

They followed Sophie down the hall, around a corner and through a curtain to where Tilda was propped up on pillows, awake, but weak.

"Mommy!"

"Baby." Emily wrapped her in a careful hug, avoiding the tubes carrying fluids and medications into her little body. "Poor Tilda. Are you feeling a little better, honey?"

"A lot," she said. But she was pale, and her eyes had bruise-like circles under them. Her voice lacked its usual energy and enthusiasm. "Can we go home now?"

Joey was standing beside the bed, and Em felt his presence like a strong and solid force, and a source of strength. He said,

"We're going to have to spend the night here, honey. But they're getting us a nice room ready right now."

"Are you staying, too?" she asked.

"Wild horses couldn't get me to leave, princess."

"So…yes?" she asked

"Yes," he said. "I'm right here. I'm not going anywhere. Not ever." And when he said it, he shifted his eyes to Emily's, and she felt his promise in that look and knew it was for her, too.

CHAPTER THIRTEEN

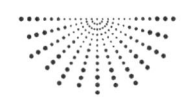

They paced. They drank coffee. Joey and Em took shifts in the room with Tilda, because the staff said they were already breaking rules by letting even one of them stay overnight. Not to mention the plethora of Brands and McIntyres in the waiting room.

Joey was currently on a break in the waiting room. He'd fallen into a pattern. Restroom, bottle of water, something to eat, talk to the family, and then relieve Emily.

Brands came and went. Two of the Texas clan had come into the waiting room and hadn't budged all night, Wes and Ben. Wes looked like he had Native American blood, long dark hair and the chiseled features of a movie star. Ben was big all over, with dirty blond hair that was bumping up against the border of shaggy. Others drifted in and out. They came and went, that sprawling crew of Texans, maybe going to their assigned beds for a couple hours of sleep before returning.

Vidalia and Bobby Joe never left the waiting room. Neither had Joey's brothers.

Vidalia's daughters were taking shifts, and whichever of them was on duty made food and beverage runs to keep everyone else going. When they came back after a break, they brought anything they'd thought of in the interim. Blankets, wet wipes, tea bags, airline pillows, you name it.

Selene was there just then, over on the waiting room sofa talking intently to Wes and Ben Brand. Nodding, she came to where Joey stood, one arm braced against the vending machine.

"I'd like you to let my cousins see Tilda," she said softly.

He looked from Selene to the two men and frowned.

"Wes is a shaman. Comanche. He's for real, Joey. He wants to do a healing on her. He can do it while she's sleeping. It won't even wake her up."

He glanced at the men, sighed. "And what about the other one? Ben?"

"He does Reiki."

He sighed. "What the hell can it hurt? I'll talk to Emily."

"Emily's all for it," she said from behind him.

He turned around. She'd pulled her long sleeved green sweater down over her hands. It made her seem small within its softness. Her posture was weak and her eyes were swollen and tired. She sent him a loving look, then went to the waiting room and spoke softly to Wes and Ben. Nodding, they got up.

Emily said, "It's this way," and she took Joey's hand on the way past. "They can throw us out if they want to. Or try. I'm going to watch. Come with me."

He fell into step beside her. They passed Vidalia, who held a tray of mugs, and Joey grabbed a couple on his way by and whispered "thank you." Everything they said was in whispers. Almost as if they had some irrational fear that speaking too loudly would anger the monster inside their little girl and somehow speed things up.

Then they stood in the doorway, side by side, watching as Wes and Ben moved silently around sweet, sleeping Tilda. Wes gestured with his hands and whispered in a kind of cadence that matched his movements. Ben sat quietly, holding his two large hands over Tilda, almost but not quite touching her. First her head, and then her face, and then her neck.

Joe put his arm around Emily and pulled her close. Bending near, he whispered, "I'm not just with you for her sake, you know. For my sake, too. That's not gonna change, Emily. No matter what."

He felt her start to tremble. "I um...I need to..." She turned, and gulped, "Stay with her, okay?" and then she headed down the hall and out through the exit doors.

~

Emily burst through the double doors into an area in the back of the hospital, clearly made for vehicles to drop off or pick up patients. She followed a sidewalk until she found a shadowy little bench to sit on.

And then she just sank down. Her body bent in on itself, and she sobbed.

Joey, assuring her that he wanted to be with her no matter what, had thrown her over a cliff into despair. Because to her, what he meant was, he would stay with her even if Tilda didn't make it. Which meant he didn't think she was going to. Which made her feel hopeless.

Her sobs came harder and harder. She thought they would rip her chest open.

And then a strong hand came to her back, and powerful arms pulled her close, and Joey whispered, "I know. I know." And then he was crying, too. And they just sat there like that, holding each other and sobbing on a dark and lonely bench, beside an overflowing ashtray with its top on crooked, beneath a broken overhead lamp. It was a dark place to cry in private, a place where countless worried parents like the two of them had probably held each other and wept.

And then a sound came floating around the back of the

hospital to that desolate bench. A magical sound that found them, even there in the depths of despair.

Voices. Voices that were singing. "Silent Night."

They pulled apart, frowning and searching each other's faces. The tears on Joey's cheeks gleamed back at her. And something in her heart melted into his. "Is she alone?" she asked. "She's not alone, is she?"

He shook his head. "I wouldn't leave her alone. Ben and Wes finished up and Vidalia asked if she could sit with her for a while." He took her hands, tugged her to her feet. "Let's see what this is all about, huh?" He held her close to his side as they walked together, farther along the sidewalk, around the side of the hospital in Big Falls' big sister town of Tucker Lake. As they turned the final corner, they saw a sea of candle flames. It was such an amazing sight, they both stopped moving and just stared.

Each dancing yellow candle lit the face of the person who held it, making them glow as they sang. It was like walking in on a choir of angels.

Joey squeezed Emily's shoulder, and they moved further around until they stood at the hospital's main entrance, where the crowd seemed to be focused. People saw them, recognized them, nodded, raised candles toward them. The singing grew louder.

Emily felt herself filing up to bursting with something as warm and alive as the golden glow of all those candles. Her tears flowed silently, tears of gratitude, and of hope, washing away her worry and grief, if only for a moment.

Joey tipped his head until it touched hers, and said, "Look, there's Vidalia's prayer group, over by the fountain."

She looked up at his face, his beautiful face, and then followed his gaze out to where the pastor and a lot of his flock, including many people she had met in Big Falls, stood in a little huddle, singing their hearts out. She recognized Ida Mae and her friend Betty Lou, and Rosie from the diner.

Then she swept her gaze out over the crowd and said, "Those must be Selene's Wiccans," nodding toward a group of girls all decked out in goth in the middle of an open patch of lawn.

"Nope," he said, and he pointed elsewhere. "Her girls are over there by the aspens."

She followed his gaze. Ordinary looking women, holding their candles and singing like the rest. Maybe they wore a little more jewelry than the others.

"There are the Texans," he said, nodding again.

That group was bigger than all the rest. She'd met most of them by now, but couldn't remember most of their names. Ben and Wes had rejoined the rest of their family, and they held candles, too. They were all there, even the children, holding those candles up and singing their hearts out.

All told, there must have been a couple of hundred people gathered in that parking lot, and all for their little girl.

Just then a clock somewhere began striking. She turned and looked up at its old-fashioned dial. Its arms both pointed straight up. Midnight.

"It's officially Christmas Eve," Joey whispered.

She leaned against him, closed her eyes and, for the first time in a long time, she prayed, "God, whoever and wherever you are, please, please, please…" Her throat closed off, and she tried to think the rest loudly enough for any higher power to hear. *Please don't take my baby from me.*

Joey's eyes were closed too, and she was pretty sure he was uttering a prayer of his own. And eventually he opened them again and said, "We should get back inside." Then he looked out at the sea of family, friends and neighbors and waved.

Emily had been wondering what one was supposed to do in the face of such overwhelming love and support. So she followed his lead and waved, too. It didn't seem like nearly enough. She didn't think all those people out there would ever know just how much their presence meant to her, just then.

"Thank you," Joey said loudly. "Thank you all so much. This is just…" He choked up.

Emily saw him struggling. "It's amazing," she said, and saw the gratitude in his eyes before focusing on the crowd again. "*You're* amazing, all of you. Thank you."

People smiled, a few clapped, several shouted.

"We love you."

"God Bless You."

"Merry Christmas."

Then the two of them turned to go back inside but were stopped when a white-coated woman with a clipboard and beautiful dark brown eyes came out, almost bumping into them. She looked at her clipboard, then in a loud voice, told the crowd, "We can take last names that begin with L through O now. L through O, come on down."

The crowd started morphing its shape as individuals made their way to the front.

Emily touched the woman's shoulder. "Excuse me, what are they—"

"You're Matilda Louise's parents," she said, apparently recognizing them.

Em nodded. "What's this list for?"

"We have almost three hundred people here, waiting for us to test them for compatibility with your little girl."

Emily blinked in shock and looked back out over that crowd. They'd restarted "Silent Night" on the third verse.

"Three hundred….?" She looked at Joey, her eyes wide.

"That's Big Falls," he said. "I know, it's surreal. I've been there two years now, and I'm still getting used to it. It's a special town, Emily. Selene says it's located on some kind of energy center. Vidalia says it's blessed by angels. Different people have different theories, but everyone pretty much agrees there's something magical about the place."

She nodded, looking one last time at the individuals who were lining up in front of the lab tech. Strangers. Young, old, teenagers, skin tones ranging the full spectrum of humanity. All of them smiling at her, touching her shoulder or Joey's as they passed. Giving them encouraging nods and telling them to hold on, hang in there, keep the faith.

"I've never seen anything like this in all my life."

He held her hand a little tighter. "I don't think there *is* anything like this." Then he walked her back inside.

---

6 :00 a.m.

When Emily came out of the restroom, Joey was waiting outside the door. He leaned back against the wall, one leg crossed over the other. He had a funny look on his face.

"I…thought you were staying with Tilda while I washed up."

He straightened. "Her grandmothers wanted some time with her."

"Oh, your mom got here?" she asked. He'd told her earlier that Judith would be here as soon as possible.

"Yeah. She'd have been here last night, but her night vision is terrible and Stu was out of town."

"Good, that's good. I'm glad she's here." She swallowed hard. "Joey…you don't think Tilda's going to…" Her voice cracked, and the question became a choked whisper.

"No." He pulled her hard into his arms, held her close, rocked her slowly. "No, Emily, I do not think that." He lifted her chin, looked into her eyes, then said, "Come on," and turning her in his arm, started walking down the hall, not in the direction of Tilda, or the waiting room, but the opposite.

"Where are we going?"

"Somewhere private. Where we can sit down and talk." He kept walking, scanning both sides of every hallway, until he saw something that made him stop and go inside.

Chapel. The sign on the door said chapel.

But it was just a room. A few chairs, a small table, a bookshelf holding the Koran, the Bible, the Torah, the Dao, and other holy books in a number of languages. There were a dozen white taper candles, all of them burned down to various heights on a metal shelf. Long wooden matchsticks lined up in front of them, and along the edge of the shelf, there were objects. Trinkets, people had left, maybe in offering. Silver coins, tiny medallions, tumbled stones. Most of the candles were already lit.

She looked at their steady flames. The moisture in her eyes making orange and yellow kaleidoscopes of their light. "I'll bet most of those are for Tilda."

"I'll bet you're right." He moved closer and picked up a match stick. "Let's light one together."

Nodding, she put her hand on top of his, and they moved the matchstick to steal a little fire from a nearby prayer, and carry it to the tallest of the few unlit candles. They touched their flame to its wick. Emily closed her eyes and wished with everything in her. "Make Tilda well," she whispered.

They drew the matchstick away, and she lowered her hand. Instead of crushing its flame out, Joey moved it to another unlighted taper, and touched its wick with the flame. "Make Emily say yes."

She frowned at him. He crushed out the burning matchstick, dropped it back where it belonged and pulled something out of his pocket. Then he dropped to one knee and gazed up at her.

"I know this might seem like bad timing, Em, but I gave it a lot of thought, and I think it's just the opposite. I need you in my life as much as I need that little girl in there. Now more than ever. I love you, Emily Hawkins. I've loved you since I was a little guy, and I imagine I'll die loving you still. I want you to marry me."

Everything inside her seemed to condense itself into a fresh batch of tears and welled and spilled over and rolled down her cheeks. "I love you, too," she said, but it came out garbled because she was crying so hard. She fell to her knees to kiss him, and their kisses tasted of tears.

Then she felt him fumbling with her left hand, and broke the kiss long enough to help. She watched in wonder as he slid a rose-tinted diamond ring surrounded by tiny blue sapphires onto her finger.

"It was my great grandmother's," he said. "I asked Mom to bring it."

"It's beautiful." The ring on her finger winked and twinkled the reflection of the dancing candles beside her.

"How's the fit?"

"Almost perfect."

He took hold of her hand, to look at the fit. "I'll have it sized."

"It's not leaving my finger," she said, pulling her hand away. Then she held her hand up and moved the ring in the candlelight to watch it shoot fire. "It's the most beautiful ring I've ever seen. Truly." Then she blinked at him and realized he'd distracted her from their vigil. Given her a moment of joy in the middle of her soul's darkest night.

"So we're really doing this? Getting married?" she asked softly.

He smiled. "We're really doing this." He sounded as surprised as she felt. But it felt good. It felt right.

He grabbed her and kissed her, and she let herself be completely engulfed in him, in the kissing, in the holding, in the sharing love to dispel, ever so briefly, the awfulness happening just beyond the chapel doors.

He lifted his head. "We're really doing this," he said, and this time he sounded confident and sure.

"We've got to tell Tilda," she said.

He took her hand, and they took a single step, then stopped at the sound of something clattering to the floor behind them.

Emily turned, frowning, to see that one of the little offerings had fallen from the metal shelf of candles, and she bent to pick it up, and then just stayed there, crouched, staring at the object she held in her hand.

"What is it, Em?" Joe came behind her as she rose.

She held the tiny figurine up. A miniature, porcelain likeness of Our Lady of Guadalupe. She stared at it, then at him. "Joey...?"

He blinked at her. "Didn't you say you left that money my father gave your father....at the Shrine of Our Lady of Guadalupe in New Mexico?"

She nodded, dumbfounded. "With a note that said, 'you owe me one.'" Again and again she looked at the lady, at the exquisite serenity in Her face. Gently, she placed Her back on the shelf, right in front of the candle she'd lit for Matilda.

Emily didn't believe in magic and miracles. If she ever had, even a little bit, that kind of thinking had been crushed the day Matilda's doctor had given her the dire diagnosis. Or so she'd thought.

But since coming to Big Falls, she'd seen things, felt things... she'd changed, she realized. Something inside her had been broken open. Some tender center she'd kept locked away since her father's death. She was different now.

Hand in hand, she and Joey left the chapel, heading back down the hall toward Tilda's room.

Sophie was in the hallway outside Tilda's door, talking to Vidalia and Judith, and all three of them were crying.

Emily's heart fell. "No," she whispered, breaking into a run. "No, no, no!"

CHAPTER FOURTEEN

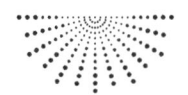

*J*oey's feet felt like lead. He tried to run, to keep up with Em as she charged toward his mom and Vidalia and Sophie, her shoes sliding on the floor when she reached them, her hands clutching Sophie's shoulders, her eyes searching her face.

"She's okay, Emily. She's okay."

Joey was suddenly able to move his feet a little faster. Emily turned to look through the glass into Tilda's room. The crushing fear on her face changed. She smiled. Her hands came to her cheeks. Then she looked his way, beaming, but still with rivers of tears.

"Joe, come look! She's sitting up, flipping channels with the remote, eyes glued to the TV screen."

He finally made it to her side, looked past her through the glass in the door. There was beautiful Tilda, her long honey and copper curls in need of brushing, working the remote like a pro. She wasn't deathly pale, and the circles under her eyes had all but vanished.

Emily covered his hand with hers, and he caressed the ring

she wore with his thumb. He heard Vidalia gasp and whisper, "Is that–?" and his mom reply, "It is."

"She looks so much better," Emily said, as if she hadn't noticed the two grandmothers noticing her ring. "What's going on, Sophie?"

"Well, it turns out that her pneumonia was not caused by Sanguis Morbo," Sophie said. "It had another source. She probably got some river water into her lungs the other day, and there's been an infection brewing ever since. IV antibiotics are taking care of it, as you can tell by looking at her. She's responding so well, she can probably go home tonight, though I'd like her to stay a few more hours just to be sure."

"Then the Sanguis Morbo hasn't become active yet, after all?" Joey asked, almost limp with relief.

"Better than that," Sophie said, smiling as those who'd been in the waiting room—and that was a lot of people now that morning had come—came crowding into the hallway. They had a clear view of Tilda's room from there, and it was obvious there was news being shared. Sophie took a beat to let them get within earshot, and speaking a little more loudly than before, said, "Matilda doesn't have Sanguis Morbo. She never had it. I've retested her three times. There's no sign of SM whatsoever."

Dead silence. No one seemed to be able to absorb that information. Joey's heart started beating so fast he thought it was going to jackhammer a hole straight through his chest.

Emily was trembling, her eyes shifting from Sophie's to his and back again. "But…but…her doctor told me… her tests showed… how can this be?"

She was afraid to believe. Joey understood it because he was, too. He put an arm around her, held her tight to his side.

"I called her doctor," Sophie went on. "Woke him up. He said this would be the fifth false positive this year from the lab he uses. Used to use, that is."

Emily's frown deepened. "It was...it was a false positive?" She looked at Joey again, searching his eyes, asking him if she could trust this. If this could be real. For the life of him, he didn't know the answer. "All we've been through was nothing more than a mistake?"

"Yes." Sophie clasped each of them by a shoulder. "Yes, Emily, it was a false positive. A lab error."

"Lab error my backside," Vidalia hooted. "It's a miracle, is what it is! Prayer works."

"I love when Reiki works so quickly," Ben Brand said, smiling Joey's way, and lifting his hand toward his closest cousin for a high five.

"Reiki, my ass," Selene said, leaving him hanging. "My Witches and I conjured the biggest healing spell you ever saw."

Wes said, "My sources say it was not her time. This was all about...something else." He nodded toward Joe and Emily, and Joey felt his face get warm.

Everyone smiled at them, so he took the moment to grab Emily's wrist and hold her hand up. "And we're engaged."

Everyone cheered, and a half dozen nurses showed up to start herding Brands and McIntyres outside. They took turns clapping Joe's shoulder or taking Emily's hand and offering congratulations.

As they all finally cleared out, Joey opened the hospital room door, and together they went in.

"What was everybody yellin' about?" Tilda asked, lifting her little hands, palms up.

"Well, for one thing," Emily said, "you are going to be all better in no time flat, and you get to come home today."

"That's good. Santa would never find me here."

"So...Tilda," Emily said, sliding up onto the bed and pulling her little girl into her arms. "What would you think about us all living together?"

"You and Daddy and me?" Tilda asked, and Em nodded. "But we already do. In the cabin, for Christmas."

"What would you think about us living together…for always?"

Tilda widened her eyes and her mouth formed an O as she looked at Joey. "Really?"

"I asked your mom to marry me. What do you think about that?"

She sprang upright and started jumping on the bed. The IV pole tipped and he lunged to catch it at the same instant Emily caught Tilda around the waist and set her gently down. Then she carefully untangled the IV lines, met his eyes, widened hers and smiled.

"I guess that means you like the idea," Joey said, moving closer to his girls.

"Did you get a ring, Mommy?"

"Mmm-hmm," she said, holding out her hand for inspection.

Tilda giggled. "Now you gotta kiss."

"Not gonna argue with the princess," Joey said, and he leaned in to kiss Emily softly on the lips. They were both smiling before they stopped clinging, and suddenly a loud cheer went up from outside the hospital.

"Apparently the news has been shared with those sitting vigil outside." He moved just far enough to crank the window open.

The cheering went on and on, and then, bit by bit, it morphed into another round of "Silent Night."

"That's gonna be my favorite Christmas song for the rest of my life," Emily said.

"Mine, too," Joey said. He sat on the opposite side of the bed, his arm around Emily with Tilda snuggled in between them. "Mine, too."

–The End–

Continue reading for an excerpt from the next book in the
McIntyre Men series,
Shine On Oklahoma.

PREVIEW SHINE ON, OKLAHOMA

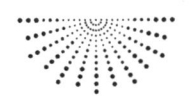

CHAPTER ONE

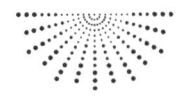

Dax Russell hit the double doors running, only to be met by a nurse and an orderly. The alarm on their faces let him know he was out of line.

He took a step back, held up his hands. "Sorry." He was out of breath, had run all the way from the taxi. Then he saw his mom, just coming out of a hospital room through a heavy wood door that dwarfed her. Caroline Russell was Tinkerbell personified, and he adored her.

She met his eyes, gave him a sad smile and then said to the staff standing between them, "It's okay. That's our son."

"Oh. Thank God." The nurse patted his chest, and the orderly grinned and shook his head as they moved aside. Dax met his mom halfway. Her pixie short platinum hair was probably mostly silver now, but you couldn't really tell with blond hair that light. She hugged him and he picked her up off her feet like he always did when he saw her. It was kind of their thing, him being so big, her being so small. He hugged her hard, but not too hard, then set her on her little feet again.

It often amazed him that a man of his size had somehow been produced by a little thing like his mom.

"How are you, honey?" she asked.

He lifted his head and looked toward the door she'd come out of. "I'll let you know."

"No, tell me now. How *are* you?"

The way she said it, he knew what she was asking. And he didn't mind. "Dry since Christmas," he said. "Not a drop."

"And?"

He smiled. "Life is pretty amazing when your eyeballs are clear enough to see it."

"It is."

It wasn't. The only woman he'd ever loved was a criminal, and he couldn't seem to get over her. But that wasn't anything his mother needed to know.

She took him by the hand, led him in the wrong direction.

He tugged half-heartedly. "I should see him."

"After we talk." She led him through the ICU, through a set of doors and into a small waiting room with little round tables and padded chairs. A TV set mounted high on one ivory wall played the headlines to no audience. A row of vending machines, a row of windows, and a water cooler filled the remaining wall space.

Caroline went to a little table far from the television, near the windows. Dax sat down, and she did too, and then she clasped his hand in both of hers across the table. "It's your father's time honey," she said. "The cardiologist is amazed he even made it to the hospital. It was a massive heart attack."

It seemed like her words didn't register in his brain at first. She could read him, his mom could. She loved him, had left her boorish husband mostly because of him, he'd always thought. His father was a bully, and it didn't matter if you were a business rival or his own son. He was mean to everyone. And yet she was here. Probably because there was no one else who cared enough to be bothered.

"He's going to die," she said. "Do you understand, Dax?"

"He's gonna die?"

"Yes. I'm sorry, son."

He blinked, trying to find words. His father was a strapping, powerful man. He couldn't just die. "When?"

"Could be any minute. Could be a couple of days. The doctor says it won't be longer. Right now, he's slipping in and out of consciousness. Eventually, he'll just slip out and keep on going."

"Wh-what about life support? Why can't they keep him—"

"There's too much damage to his heart, Dax. He'd need a transplant, but there's damage to other organs, as well, and his lifetime of drinking has riddled his liver. There's no way back from this."

He blinked, taking that in. It sounded cold, somehow. "Can I see him now?" he asked, staring at nothing, a spot in the space between them.

She nodded and let go of his hand. "I'll be right here."

He got to his feet and walked mindlessly out of the waiting room. A nurse saw him, the one who'd stopped him in the hall, and gave a smile. He had brown hair and bangs that tried to cover up the acne on his forehead, and his eyes were soft but knowing. He pointed at the door, and said, "three-oh-five" in a funeral voice.

Dax pushed the door open and went inside. At first he thought he'd walked into the wrong room. A wrinkled, saggy-faced man with gray tinted skin lay against white sheets, beneath a white blanket. The top sheet was folded over the blanket, and the old man's arms were resting on top of it. There was an IV line in his arm, and oxygen tubes in his nostrils. There were leads strung from his chest to a monitor. The monitor and IV were mounted to a pole beside the bed. The oxygen came from a port on the wall.

His hair was mostly white, but streaks of carrot-stained

yellow still showed through. That was what told Dax he wasn't in the wrong room, those faded orange streaks. Only he used to have a lot more of them.

When did he get so old?

Dax sank into a bedside chair and remembered the last time he'd spoken to his father. He'd admitted that he'd taken money from the Aurora Downs accounts to give to a beautiful con artist for a kidney transplant she didn't really need. He'd paid it back, thanks to a loan from a friend. But that hadn't mattered to his father. He'd fired him on the spot, called him six kinds of idiot, and disowned him.

That had been eighteen months ago.

Mom was sure he'd been sorry after. She thought Dax ought to come home and talk it out. But he knew better. Dax had apologized three times, deeply and sincerely, in voicemails left on his father's cell, because the old man wouldn't take his calls. But admitting he'd been even a little bit wrong was beneath the great man. In fact, sitting there, Dax couldn't recall ever hearing his father apologize to anyone in his whole life. Still, he wished they'd made peace, him and Dad, before it came to this.

"I thought there'd be more time." Dax said it softly, turning away, blinking back tears. He focused on the monitor instead of the man, studied its wavy lines and numbers as if he had a clue what they meant.

"*Now* you show up."

Dax turned fast, saw that the old man's eyes were open, watery and bloodshot, the white parts tarnished. "Dad." He moved closer, patted a big hand with his own. "I'm here."

His father grimaced, then his eyes fell closed. "I thought so, too," he said.

"Thought what, too?" Dax recalled his own words. "That there'd be more time?"

His father nodded.

"It doesn't matter now, Dad. It's all good, all is forgiven."

Those dull eyes popped open with near violent force and his head came right off the pillow. *"Forgiven?"* There was no mistaking the disgust in his voice. Then he let his head fall back onto the pillows again. "Nothing is forgiven. I thought there'd be more time to change my will. Too late now, though."

Dax stood up slow, knowing now that this wasn't going to be the moment he'd wanted it to be. No mending of the rift, no healing moment, no tender goodbye. He was stupid to have thought it could be like that. Then he took a deep breath. "I'm sorry about what I did. I honestly thought Kendra's life depended on it."

"She played you."

"It's what she does." He shrugged. "I thought you'd want to make peace with your only son before you died. I thought you'd want a chance to say goodbye."

His father closed his eyes. "Try not to fuck up my legacy like you fuck up everything else."

It stung. It shouldn't have. He'd hardened his heart against his old man years ago. And yet it stung. "If you left it to me, you can forget it. I don't want it."

His father's eyes opened a little wider. "You refuse it, it goes to the SRA."

"I don't care. Let the State Racing Association have it."

"But your mother…"

"Owns forty-nine percent. I know. She can do what she wants with her half. It has nothing to do with me." He started to turn away, but a hand gripped his wrist with surprising strength. He turned back. His father's face wasn't white, it was red, bordering on purple, his eyes bulging.

"She'll go to prison."

Dax widened his eyes. "What did you do, Dad?"

"SRA…the books…" He relaxed all at once. His eyes fell closed.

Dax swore, and bent over his father, clasped his shoulders. "What about the books? Dad! Dad!"

His father didn't reply. His face didn't look strained anymore. It was relaxed. Dax shot a look at the monitor. Its lines had gone flat.

Shine On Oklahoma

ALSO AVAILABLE

The McIntyre Men
Oklahoma Christmas Blues
Oklahoma Moonshine
Oklahoma Starshine
Shine On Oklahoma
Baby By Christmas
Oklahoma Sunshine

The Oklahoma Brands
The Brands who Came for Christmas
Brand-New Heartache
Secrets and Lies
A Mommy For Christmas
One Magic Summer
Sweet Vidalia Brand

ABOUT THE AUTHOR

New York Times and *USA Today* bestselling novelist Maggie Shayne has published sixty-two novels and twenty-two novellas for five major publishers over the course of twenty-two years. She also spent a year writing for American daytime TV dramas *The Guiding Light* and *As the World Turns*, and was offered the position of co-head writer of the former; a million-dollar offer she tearfully turned down. It was scary, turning down an offer that big. But her heart was in her books, and she'd found it impossible to do both.

In March 2014, she did something even scarier. She left the world's largest publisher and went "indie."

Now, she is embarking on an exciting new leg of her publishing journey, with most of her titles moving to small press publisher, Oliver Heber Books.

Maggie writes small town contemporary romances like the recent *Bliss in Big Falls* series, which boasts "a miracle in every story."

She cut her teeth on western themed category romances like her classic 90s and early 2000s *The Texas Brand* and *The Oklahoma All-Girl Brands,* and later expanded into romantic suspense and thrillers like *The Secrets of Shadow Falls* and *The Brown and de Luca Novels*.

She is perhaps best known for her beloved paranormal romances, like the brand new *Fatal series* and perennial favorites *The Immortals*, the *By Magic series*, and *Wings in the Night*.

Maggie is a fifteen-time RITA® Award nominee and one-time winner. She lives in the rolling green and forested hilltops of Cortland County NY, wine & dairy country, despite having sworn off both. She is a vegan Wiccan hippy living her best life with her beloved husband Lance, and usually at least two dogs.

Maggie also writes spiritual self-help and runs an online magic shop, BlissBlog.org

Visit Maggie at www.maggieshayne.com

Lightning Source UK Ltd.
Milton Keynes UK
UKHW041110130223
416849UK00004B/65